*A Candlelight
Ecstasy Romance*®

"I WANT AN EXPLANATION. WHY DIDN'T YOU TELL ME THE TRUTH ABOUT YOUR IDENTITY? WHY COULDN'T YOU TRUST ME?"

Sarah hesitated. Had she really meant something special to him, or had his feelings just been hurt by the deception? She lifted her chin defiantly. "I don't owe you anything, Tyler. You never led me to believe that you wanted any more from me than a few nights of diversion."

"You know it was more than that. As soon as I realized what kind of person you were underneath those gaudy wigs and flashy clothes, I knew what I was feeling for you was more than I should."

"You could have told me that," she murmured.

"And you could have told me who you were."

CANDLELIGHT ECSTASY ROMANCES®

ANOTHER SUNNY DAY

Kathy Clark

A CANDLELIGHT ECSTASY ROMANCE®

Published by
Dell Publishing Co., Inc.
1 Dag Hammarskjold Plaza
New York, New York 10017

Dell ® TM 681510, Dell Publishing Co., Inc.
Candlelight Ecstasy Romance®, 1,203,540, is a registered
trademark of Dell Publishing Co., Inc., New York, New York.

ISBN: 0-440-10202-2

Printed in the United States of America
First printing—February 1985

To my most loyal fan, best friend, most diligent helper, and the person who made me what I am—my mother, Betty Jones

To Our Readers:

We have been delighted with your enthusiastic response to Candlelight Ecstasy Romances®, and we thank you for the interest you have shown in this exciting series.

In the upcoming months we will continue to present the distinctive sensuous love stories you have come to expect only from Ecstasy. We look forward to bringing you many more books from your favorite authors and also the very finest work from new authors of contemporary romantic fiction.

As always, we are striving to present the unique, absorbing love stories that you enjoy most—books that are more than ordinary romance.

Your suggestions and comments are always welcome. Please write to us at the address below.

Sincerely,

The Editors
Candlelight Romances
1 Dag Hammarskjold Plaza
New York, New York 10017

CHAPTER ONE

Sarah blinked her sleepy blue eyes in confusion. The hotel room looked like hundreds of others she had slept in, and after seven years it took longer to clear the cobwebs from her mind each morning. She squinted at the small luminous dial of her travel alarm clock. It was several seconds before the time came into focus, and with a groan she burrowed deeper under the covers and hugged her pillow tightly against her ears.

From the voices filtering through her closed door she knew it must be her identical twin sister, the popular country and western singer, Sunny Day, returning from another of the many late night parties that she had been attending lately. Sarah also recognized the brisk baritone of her sister's manager, Mack. Sarah didn't enjoy the after-hours social life that had become so important to Sunny, and frequently, as she had tonight, she left early and came back to the hotel alone, going to bed in an attempt to catch up on the rest that was so difficult to get during their exhausting road trips.

But nothing she did could drown out the loud discussion that penetrated the hotel's thin walls. The more she tried to ignore the noise, the more irritating it got until, with a bang, her door burst open, the blinding overhead light was switched on, and two bodies simultaneously bounced in, one on each side of her bed.

"Mack, there is nothing you can say or do to me that will get me on horseback ever again." Sunny's voice was shrill, almost hysterical. "There are other jobs and other cities where I can sing without ever having to see or smell another horse." She wrinkled her small pert nose delicately.

"Sure, if you think that you'll get rich and famous playing such small towns as DeRidder, Louisiana, or Duncan, Oklahoma, then you don't need me as your manager; you need a psychiatrist," Mack said with a snort. "If you miss this gig in Houston, you won't have any choice but to sing at school assemblies and supermarket openings. No one else will touch you. Let me remind you that you're under contract to appear at the opening night performance of the Houston Livestock Show and Rodeo as the headliner. You were booked five months ahead of time. They couldn't possibly find a suitable replacement on such short notice, not to mention all the bad publicity you'd get for canceling another performance. You're getting a reputation for missing as many as you make lately." He spoke honestly and harshly, thinking it would be better to hurt her feelings than to let her ruin her career.

"In case you two haven't noticed"—Sarah threw off her pillow and sat up, pushing her long disheveled blond hair off her face—"it's *only* two o'clock in the morning,

10

and *someone* in this room is trying to get some sleep, and at this moment she is not having much success. I don't mean to sound unfriendly or unsympathetic," she added pointedly, "but couldn't this conversation be held somewhere else at some other time, and preferably without me?"

The two intruders barely glanced her way before continuing as if she had never spoken.

"It's not the rodeo I'm dreading," Sunny moaned. "It's that darn trail ride and parade. I couldn't live through all that riding and being outside all day with all those horses. Ugh!"

"I asked you about all of that before you signed the contract, and it didn't seem to bother you then. What's the big deal about it now?" Mack was totally exasperated with his client. Lately her temperament was outweighing her talent, which made his job much more difficult.

"Five months ago I was thinking about all of that free publicity and all those gorgeous cowboys. You know that I can't resist a real live cowboy, especially the home-grown Texas variety." Her thick false eyelashes fluttered expressively. "Besides, that was before that horse in Billings mistook my costume for lunch and before that other horse in Dubuque turned left and I turned right. I was black and blue for a month, not to mention my wounded pride. It was very humiliating out there in that arena, one minute waving at my adoring fans and the next minute lying face down in horse manure, dirt, and sawdust."

"You certainly got a lot of free publicity from that

performance!" Sarah chimed in, only to be silenced by a stony glare from her sister.

"That is not the type of publicity or treatment a star of my stature deserves," Sunny said with a haughty sniff.

"You forgot the time that horse in Tucson stepped on your foot and wouldn't move. You lost all your toenails and had to wear open-toed boots for months," Sarah added, getting into the spirit of the conversation with her unwelcome reminder.

"No one will ever convince me that that horse didn't step on me on purpose. He looked me straight in the eye, and I swear he smiled. They are vicious animals."

"Maybe they prefer rock and roll, or maybe they're music critics," Sarah teased.

Mack struggled to regain control of the situation. "Sunny, you have got to overcome your 'horse complex' for a few days and get through this. The promoter promised you a job in Las Vegas if you can prove you are still a big enough draw to fill the Houston Astrodome. They have guaranteed that you will get the best of care and a whole army of big, handsome cowboys for bodyguards. All you have to do is put in a daily appearance and let the local television stations and newspapers take a few pictures of you riding merrily along or sitting by a cozy campfire acting like you are having the time of your life."

"That's easy for you to say," Sunny declared hotly. "You'll be in some hotel sleeping on a soft bed, taking it easy, with no horse teeth or horse feet or hard horse saddles anywhere in sight while I'm being horribly tortured in front of millions of Americans on the six o'clock

12

news." She sighed dramatically. "I've been working too hard, and I'm just not up to this job. They'll have to find someone else."

"But they're expecting you—the great Sunny Day," Mack reminded her again. "It's just too bad there aren't two of you. . . ."

Silence filled the small room as Sunny and Mack turned toward Sarah, who had been sitting with her arms wrapped around her pulled up knees, watching the scenario unfold around her. Through narrowed eyes she looked suspiciously from one innocent-looking face to the other.

"Why do I get the feeling that I have been set up for this little performance? Well, you two connivers have been wasting your time, because I'm going back to sleep." Sarah lay down. "And turn the lights out when you leave," she added as she pulled the blanket over her head.

"Oh, no, you don't." Sunny yanked the blanket off her sister's curled up body. "This is so perfect I can't believe we didn't think of it sooner."·

"You probably did," Sarah muttered, but Sunny continued enthusiastically.

"You love horses and getting up early—"

"Not this early!"

". . . eating beans out of a can and sleeping under the stars. You were always after Dad to take you camping when we were kids. Now you can pretend to be me getting the star treatment and have a well-deserved vacation at the same time."

13

"Oh, sure. And then when I get in front of thirty thousand people at the Astrodome and start to sing, your career will *really* be over, because instead of buying your records the audience will be throwing them—at me," Sarah pointed out.

Sarah could always be counted on to be the sensible sister. Their mother had often said that when they were born, Sunny got all the talent, Sarah got all the brains, and the beauty was distributed evenly between them. Sarah could no more imitate Sunny's magical voice than Sunny could coordinate a road tour or handle the large volume of fan mail.

A frown crossed Sunny's perfect face, then disappeared. "That's no problem. You can ride on the trail ride and in the parade, and then we'll make the grand switch, and I'll do the show at the rodeo. No one will ever be the wiser."

"It just might work at that," Mack contributed. "Sunny could use the time to rest her vocal cords and get her act together so we won't be coming up with this problem again anytime soon."

"I never realized you two were such talented con artists. How long did it take you to work up this little performance?" Sarah asked incredulously. "Well, if you want my opinion, which I seriously doubt, I think that all those late nights and loud music have finally scrambled your brains, because if you think this crazy scheme would work, then you've both lost whatever good sense I gave you credit for having!"

14

"Oh, please, Sarah," Sunny pleaded. "I know that I really owe you a lot for all the things you've done for me for the last few years—actually all my life—but this is really important to me. You know how long I've wanted to play Vegas, and if you'll do this one teeny little favor for me, I promise I won't get myself into this situation ever again." She paused to catch her breath, trying to look as pitiful and helpless as possible, knowing that Sarah had always been a sucker for anyone or anything in trouble.

Sarah, however, was on to this trick. Sunny might be able to play little games with someone else, but certainly not with her twin sister, who had shared and taken part in every aspect of her life since their conception in their mother's womb. But even knowing she was being used as an accomplice in a possibly awkward situation, Sarah was tempted.

With every passing day in another different city she was becoming more dissatisfied with the kind of life she was leading. Her sister was building her career and doing something that, with only a few exceptions, she really enjoyed. But show business was not Sarah's idea of a perfect life-style. Her idea of heaven was a peaceful day outdoors, preferably on horseback, with human companionship at a minimum. Maybe this brief masquerade was just what the doctor had ordered: a vacation away from the daily pressures and schedules with nothing more important to worry about than avoiding saddle sores.

But could she get away with it? It had been many years

since she and Sunny had played this little game with their friends, teachers, and sometimes even their parents. Oddly enough, the two young girls had almost always gotten by without discovery. The bond between the sisters had remained strong through the years, but their own personalities had differentiated and become more defined as they grew older. It would certainly be embarrassing if she failed to succeed with this pretense, and the bad publicity could be devastating to Sunny's career. But both women could use the break in routine.

"Okay, I'll go along with this little scheme of yours under one condition," Sarah said finally, waving back Sunny's attempt to ecstatically hug her. "Hear me out on this, because I mean what I'm about to say.

"I'm not completely sure I can carry this masquerade off without being caught, but I'll do my best. The favor I want from you in return is my freedom. Sunny, I want you to take this time off to get your life enough under control so you won't need me to follow you around on any more of your road trips. I want to settle down and have a home base, not live out of a suitcase in a lonely hotel room for the rest of my life."

"But, I couldn't," Sunny gasped.

"No *buts*. I need to build a life of my own, and now is as good a time as any. I can buy a little place near Dad and Mom in Lexington with the money I've saved." Her large aquamarine-colored eyes filled with tears at the thought of the ties she was attempting to sever. "I'll miss you like I would miss my left arm, but it's time we tried to make it on our own."

The two sisters fell into a tearful embrace while Mack looked on, his own eyes suspiciously moist. The agreement was reached and sealed, with only the details of the changeover yet to be worked out.

Much later that day the two sisters stood before the large full-length mirrors in Sunny's hotel suite. The reflections shining back at them would have caused any unsuspecting bystander to do a double take. Except for the different costumes the young women looked identical. Both had the same smooth perfect features, which were dominated by huge expressive eyes that were a most unusual shade of bright blue with just a hint of green, set in a thick fringe of dark lashes. Sarah had kept her hair its natural shade of dark honey-gold, but Sunny had lightened hers several shades to a pale shimmering blond and had dozens of wigs to match, one of which now covered Sarah's own pinned up locks. Sunny had helped Sarah apply the heavy makeup that the singer never appeared in public without, and had chosen an outfit from the closetful in her room. The effect was so eerie that Sarah had to reach out and touch her image, as if to identify herself in the mirror.

Mack came barreling into the room. "Sunny, here's your airline ticket to Nashville, and I have Sarah's tickets to Houston—" He froze in his tracks, his mouth dropping open in amazement as he caught sight of the twins.

17

His outstretched hand holding Sunny's tickets hesitated first in front of her, then swung to Sarah.

"I can't believe it. I never realized the resemblance was so strong. I honestly can't tell you apart." He shook his head and laughed. "Sarah, whoever you are, are you absolutely positive you can't sing? We could be making twice as much money."

The women exchanged glances and giggled. They had gotten this sort of reaction often when they were children, and old memories, almost forgotten, flashed through their minds.

"When do you breathe?" Sarah ran her hand over her skin-tight stretch pants.

"These clothes may take a little getting used to, but without the flashy outfits I would be just another church choir singer waiting to be noticed. Besides, you know the old saying that a sexy woman is one who wears her clothes so tight that a man can hardly breathe!" Sunny was only half joking.

"I doubt if I can even bend my knees enough to mount a horse. And this wig is like wearing a bathing cap all the time, not to mention that my face feels like it could crack into a million pieces and fall off onto the floor at any minute."

Sunny laughed at her sister's dismayed expression. "After a little more practice you'll look and feel like an old pro. You might even want to have a few singing lessons and take Mack up on his offer to hit the road with me," she teased. "You always have been too conservative.

Maybe this experience will give you a chance to loosen up and have some fun."

"Your idea of fun and my idea of fun apparently are two very different things," Sarah declared as she reached eagerly for her faded, well-worn jeans. She had only a few more hours to be herself before she began her new role as Sunny Day.

CHAPTER TWO

Sarah knew she had been manipulated; not maliciously but effectively pushed into a situation that was awkward at best and completely humiliating at worst.

She had always traveled with Sunny, but Sunny cast a large shadow that caused everyone in her entourage to be outshone by her brilliance. It soon became evident that traveling with a superstar and actually being a superstar were two entirely different experiences. The airplane had barely lifted off the runway and the Fasten Your Seat Belts sign blinked off before her fellow passengers, hesitantly at first, found an excuse to approach her, requesting her autograph on any object that was handy, from a cocktail napkin to a plaster cast on one man's broken arm. Sarah smilingly obliged, even accepting a couple of good-natured kisses from overardent fans. Sometime after the first hour, however, the novelty wore off, and she escaped for a few minutes of quiet in the tiny restroom.

The face staring back at her from the mirror looked familiar, but not like herself. Sarah had always admired Sunny's dazzling beauty and flamboyance but had never envied it. It was amazing how a fluffy blond wig and heavy but attractive makeup could change a very pretty all-American girl into a beautiful celebrity, beloved, or at least recognized, by almost everyone. The silliness of the situation struck her, and she made an ugly face at her reflection, then giggled at the undignified image.

It was a relief when the seat belt sign again lit up and people returned to their seats. The twinkling lights of Houston stretched out for miles below them as the plane circled the airport before touching down on the runway. The stewardess graciously allowed Sarah to leave the plane first. She exited through the extended covered hall-way, looking for the representative of the Houston Rodeo Association who was to meet her here and escort her to the trail ride's beginning site.

What she wasn't expecting was the crowd of cheering fans that immediately grouped around her. Apparently the advance publicity had been a resounding success, because it seemed that half of Harris County must be packed into the stuffy waiting room, all armed with cam-eras that flashed directly into her eyes, causing her to be momentarily blinded by dozens of bright tiny stars.

It was impossible to acknowledge all the shouted greet-ings and requests as faceless hands grabbed her clothes, pulling and tugging until she was sure she would be torn apart. Swallowing back waves of hysteria, she tried to keep smiling in spite of her increasing terror. There was no shore in sight across the wide sea of demanding faces, and her progress had been completely halted. Uniformed guards attempted vainly to control the crowd, but things had already gotten out of hand.

Out of the corner of her eye Sarah noticed a tall man, his strikingly handsome face partially hidden in the shadow of a gray cowboy hat, pushing through the crowd toward her. She heard his deep voice through the crowd noise as he leaned close to her ear to announce, "I'm Tyler Ross from the Rodeo Association. Come with me."

"Gladly! I'll follow you anywhere. Just take me away from this madhouse."

Instead of allowing her to trail behind him he wrapped a steel-hard arm around her slim shoulders and sheltered her much smaller, trembling body with his own as he propelled her masterfully through the crowd, succeeding where the guards had failed to make a path when none seemed possible. In spite of the pandemonium and flash-bulbs that still twinkled around her like Christmas tree lights, she experienced a feeling of security, which was being provided by the strength and masculinity that emanated from this man. Without resistance she accepted his assistance, thankful beyond words that he was with her, escorting her through the mass of grasping fans as they slowly made their way to the central terminal of the airport.

Without pausing at the luggage area he continued through the lobby and out the glass doors to the parking lot, where a candy-apple-red Mercedes sat waiting, its motor purring expectantly. A porter stood next to the open front door, and Sarah climbed in gracefully. Tyler shut her door and after passing the porter a tip, walked around the sleek car to get in on the driver's side. They then drove off smoothly into the night.

"My luggage?" she asked.

"It's in the trunk. You should be used to special service at airports." His rich baritone drifted through the semi-darkness of the car's interior, but his sharp questioning look made Sarah realize her mistake.

Sunny had never given her luggage a second thought except for the time she went to Cheyenne and all her clothes went to Buffalo. A frantic shopping trip had ensued, and Sarah had added keeping up with all the luggage to her list of duties as Sunny's assistant.

Just now, though, Sarah had accidentally slipped back into her own identity. Her question had been an automatic response, but it was definitely not in character for Sunny Day. She would have to be more careful, but for now it was a good time to change the subject and hope Tyler Ross wouldn't give her little lapse another thought.

"I guess I should have asked you for some identification," she commented casually, gazing curiously at the masculine profile. Her open scrutiny of his face revealed little as the flash of passed streetlights briefly bathed his strong features. "But frankly I was so glad to be rescued, I would have welcomed Attila the Hun. Where is the cavalry when you really need them?" she quipped.

He glanced at her without comment, then leaned over and flipped open the glove compartment. Inside among the usual pile of papers and maps was a laminated badge, which he handed to her; he then turned on the overhead light so she could read it.

Trying to conceal her interest, she swiftly skimmed

23

through the succinct description typed beneath a tiny color photograph:

HOUSTON LIVESTOCK SHOW AND RODEO
CHAIRMAN, TRAIL RIDE COMMITTEE

NAME: Tyler Ross	AGE: 31
HEIGHT: 6'3"	WEIGHT: 190 lbs.
HAIR: Black	EYES: Gray

Nonchalantly she tossed the badge back into the glove compartment and closed the door. The picture really did not do him justice, she thought after sneaking a subtle look at her silent companion. It would have been impossible to capture on film the powerful charisma that radiated from him. Her nostrils were filled with the enticing smell of his clean, spicy after-shave, which made her acutely aware of him as a man. Sarah knew that if Sunny had known her escort would be this gorgeous Texas hunk, she would have reconsidered her position on horsing around!

The picture, however, proved that a friendly smile could crack through the dark stony expression that had been on his face since she had met him. Tiny lines fanned out from the corners of his eyes, evidence that this man laughed often. But for some reason, whenever he looked at her, she was chilled by the cold indifference of his eyes.

Why, when she felt this strong attraction to him, was he treating her so impersonally? This was certainly not the way most red-blooded males reacted to Sunny Day,

24

the star. Could it be that she was not convincing enough in her new identity? Nervously Sarah spoke. "I really should be accustomed to all that attention by now, but large crowds still frighten me."

He reproved her as he flipped off the map light. "You should know better than to travel alone. A pro like you should know what to expect."

Sarah was not at all sure how to interpret his attitude but decided to overlook the undercurrent of hostility.

"My sister and the band usually travel with me, but they all needed a vacation, so I insisted they take the time off for a little R and R. They'll be joining me when I get back to Houston. Besides, I'm a big girl and can take care of myself."

"So I noticed!" he snorted. "You were almost being loved to death when I arrived at the airport."

"Adoration of the masses is not all it's made out to be," she commented wryly, then added with a smile, "I never dreamed my knight would be wearing jeans and a cowboy hat instead of shining armor."

"Just doing my job," he said, cutting her off shortly. "Which reminds me, would you like to stop somewhere for dinner, or did you eat on the plane?"

The butterflies in her stomach had not settled down long enough for her to want to feed them. "Go ahead and stop if you want something to eat, but don't on my account. The food on the plane wasn't half-bad."

"Which also means it wasn't half-good either."

"That's true," she agreed with a grin. "I guess I wasn't very hungry."

"Well, I've already eaten, too, so I guess we'll wait until breakfast."

They drove along the wide, busy expressway for several miles in silence.

"I've always heard that Houston has an impressive and unique skyline, but I've never had the opportunity to see it at night," she commented, trying to break the heavy silence. She gazed in awe at the twinkling lights of the tall skyscrapers as they rose majestically out of the flat prairie and pierced the blue-black night sky.

"Haven't you ever performed in Houston before?" he asked flatly.

"Just twice; once at a gigantic club called Gilley's in Pasadena, and once at the Summit. But both times we came in on our tour bus during the daytime, and I guess I just wasn't paying much attention to the scenery. We've also played Dallas several times and a few other cities in Texas. But in this business there never seems to be time in our hectic schedule for sight-seeing."

"Is that why you chose to join our trail ride?" One of his dark eyebrows rose cynically. "You planning on seeing some real Texas sights . . . or becoming a sight to be seen?"

"A little of both" was her honest reply. "The publicity is priceless, and I do need a change of scenery, not to mention a good old-fashioned vacation."

"Why not the Caribbean or Europe? A trail ride is not very glamorous or luxurious, especially this time of year. February weather in this part of Texas can be very unpredictable."

26

"After a couple of days in Denver, this feels like springtime," she replied, unperturbed. "I won't even have to use my coat if it stays this warm."

"Don't count on it. We've never had a warm, dry trail ride yet. I hope you won't regret your decision to join us. However, we will keep our part of the agreement and make you as comfortable as possible. We don't usually attract the jet set, though."

"Me? A jetsetter? My sister would get a good laugh if she heard you call me that." Sarah chuckled.

"You do get around."

She looked at him sharply. "Yes, we do travel a lot, but I have never 'gotten around' like I think you mean. And if you think I'm a jetsetter because we move from city to city often, then you have obviously never traveled across America by bus several times a year. It is certainly an experience you can't forget, and I don't mean because of the scenery."

"By the time this trail ride is over, you'll welcome the comfort and convenience of a bus. That is, if you make it through the trail ride," he said challengingly.

"You don't have to worry about me. I will make it all the way to Houston, and I will keep up with everybody else," she retorted hotly. Uneasily she fingered one of the loose silvery blond curls of the suffocating wig. Suddenly she felt very tired.

"What city are we passing through now?" she asked, noticing another group of tall, well-lit buildings in the distance.

"We're still in Houston," he replied. "You're looking at

the Galleria area, which is just another overgrown office and shopping complex. Houston just keeps on growing up and out."

"We've been traveling for almost an hour and we're not even out of Houston?" she exclaimed in astonishment. "How much longer before we get to the camp?"

"If we can ever get out of this Sunday night traffic, it will only take us about two hours, more or less."

"You're joking!"

"No. The trail ride always begins in Cat Spring, which is about fifty miles from Houston. It would sort of defeat our purpose if the ride began in Houston, don't you think?" he added condescendingly.

"And I guess there are no airports any closer."

"Oh, sure, but the connections are so bad that you might have ended up in Mexico. Besides, I was heading that way myself, and since I am going to be responsible for your welfare for the next week, I was volunteered to personally escort you there."

His tone and choice of words made it clear that had he had any say in the matter, the outcome would have been different. Sarah decided conversation was not worth the effort and shifted around to a more comfortable position on the rich leather seat. In spite of the stiffness of the tight, hot pink pantsuit, which seemed to glow even in the car's darkness, she soon nodded off into a half-sleep.

The sudden silence as the engine was turned off and the irritating blink of a flashing sign awoke her, and she sat up with a start.

"Why are we stopping here?" Sarah stared doubtfully

28

at the sign proclaiming that this was the Countryside Motel.

"We're in Sealy, which is only about eight miles from Cat Spring. We're going to spend the night here and catch up with the others on the trail tomorrow." Tyler unfolded his large frame from the car and came around to open the door for her.

"I think we should go on to Cat Spring tonight. I'm not too tired, and maybe it would be better if we left with the others in the morning." She spoke nervously, intimidated by this unfriendly giant who loomed over her as she sat on the low seat.

"After a day on the trail you'll appreciate having had one extra night in a motel. Besides, there's always enough confusion the first morning without you adding to it. There'll be plenty of time for you to bask in all your glory later in the week."

"That's not what I was concerned about!" she protested.

"What is it, then?" he questioned as he reached down and offered his hand to help her out of the car.

"Nothing." Reluctantly she accepted his assistance and followed him to one of the rooms, not at all sure what to expect next.

"I registered yesterday," he explained as he opened the door and stepped back for her to enter first. "I hope you don't mind that I didn't use your real name. I, for one, don't need the hassle tonight."

"What name did you use? Mr. and Mrs. John Smith?" she inquired pointedly.

29

"So that's what's got you all lathered up!" He snorted, as if such an idea were ludicrous. "No, Miss Day. This is your own private room, fully equipped with double locks. My room is next door, and there are no connecting passageways. Rest assured that your virtue is safe with me."

Crimson ran up her neck and face as her mind scrambled for a snappy retort, but, of course, none came. No doubt several brilliant remarks would keep her awake later that night, but all she could do now was brush stiffly past him and into her clean but impersonal motel room.

"I'll get your luggage out of the car," he offered.

"All I need is my overnight bag and the garment bag. I hope that won't be too much of a bother."

"At your service, ma'am." And with a slight tip of his hat he left the room.

Inwardly fuming, she thought he had to be one of the rudest men she had ever had the misfortune to meet. She wondered if he treated everyone with so little regard, or if she was receiving special treatment. Too bad his personality didn't match his appearance. The combination of masculine charm and his virile good looks would have been irresistible. With a silent vow not to let this cowboy ruin her week, she went into the bathroom and turned on the tap in the shower.

There was a sharp knock on the outside door, and she called over the noise of the running water, "Come in. Just leave the bags on the bed and lock the door as you leave."

After a few seconds she heard the door shut again and, satisfied that she was alone at last, started to undress. With a sigh of pure pleasure she pulled the pale pink cowboy boots off and wiggled her toes, then peeled the tight pants off and tossed them on top of the boots. Blindly she struggled with a stubborn hook on the back of the pink blouse, but it was hopelessly tangled in a loop of the intricate beadwork.

"Darn these stupid clothes," she muttered, her head bent forward and the synthetic curls covering her face.

"And darn this wig." She stumbled back into the bedroom. Pulling out the pins, she yanked it off, releasing her own honey-blond hair to tumble down well past her shoulders, almost to her waist. Leisurely she combed through its length with her fingers and pushed it back out of her face as she raised her head, only to stare straight into a pair of silver-gray eyes. It was difficult to say who was more shocked, she because he was still in the room, or Tyler as he gaped openly at her.

"I suppose you have a good reason"—he shook his dark head in apparent bewilderment—"but I can't for the life of me understand why you would want to cover all that pretty hair, especially with that *thing.*" He motioned to the wig that now hung forgotten from her limp fingers, looking like a dead furry creature.

"It's really none of your business," she said defensively, her guard down. "But this wig and these clothes are all part of a carefully calculated image that sells tickets and records."

"What clothes?" his eyes roamed boldly over her long, shapely bare legs, rested briefly on her tiny bikini panties, then moved up the snug blouse to her flaming face.

Sarah struggled to regain her poise and not allow her

31

feet to let her flee to the safety and privacy of the bathroom. Instead she stood casually, trying to pretend that there was nothing unusual about her standing half-naked in a strange hotel room with an unbelievably handsome but unbearably insolent cowboy.

"The clothes I wore on the plane." Her chin lifted defiantly. "I was nobody until I put on this wig. Now it's what the public expects . . . and gets."

With a shrug of his broad shoulders he indicated that it was of no importance to him and turned to leave.

"While you're here," she said, hating to ask, "would you mind helping me with these hooks? This blouse is like a suit of armor, and I'd prefer not spending the night in it."

She pulled her long hair over one shoulder and turned her back toward him, daring him to refuse. He didn't.

The warmth of his hands burned through the cloth as if it weren't there. Agilely his large fingers loosened the hook, then slowly slid the zipper down, his light touch leaving a sensual trail in its wake.

Alarmed, she twisted her head around and looked up into his face, which was much nearer than she had expected. She felt a rush of his warm breath dancing on her cheek and the sudden tightening of his hands on her shoulders. For a long moment their gazes were locked, his look puzzled and confused, hers searching for the answer to a question she did not know. Strange electric tingles raced through her body, and her heart beat a wild rhythm against her rib cage as she watched his head bend slowly toward her, his lips nearing hers . . . almost touching.

Abruptly he moved away, his hands falling from her shoulders as if he, too, had felt the current. He put the distance of the small room between them before stopping. "I stayed to tell you that I requested wake-up calls at seven o'clock in the morning. I'll come by at eight. Will that be all right with you?"

Mutely she nodded, and he left, this time shutting the door firmly behind him. For several seconds Sarah stood alone in the middle of the room, one hand clutching the loose blouse to her chest while the tousled wig still dangled from the other. Tyler Ross definitely had an attitude problem, but she sensed that beneath that brusque, rude exterior he could be a likable person; perhaps, if that strange attraction she had felt a few moments ago was any indication, too likable. It would not be in her best interests or Sunny's to get involved, even temporarily, with anyone she met during the next week.

A cloud of steam floated from the bathroom, reminding her that she'd left the water running in the shower. With a fresh resolve to carry off this charade without further complications, Sarah finished undressing and hurried back to the shower.

CHAPTER THREE

Sarah had been awake for almost an hour the next morning when the telephone rang with her wake-up call. It had taken her almost that long to restore the wig to something resembling a hairpiece. Somehow she knew Sunny would not appreciate any publicity she got if she looked as if she had a very sick poodle on her head.

After a wistful thought about the comfortable faded jeans she usually wore, Sarah chose another of Sunny's costumes from the garment bag. The rest of the week she would wear designer jeans with a fancy blouse, but for her first appearance she thought it appropriate to make a grand entrance.

This outfit was a bright blue-green, almost the same shade as her eyes. Rhinestones were sprinkled in a starburst pattern on the back and front yokes with a long, thin silver fringe shimmering below the double stitching and hanging from both cuffs. The material itself was a soft satin, with the tight pants of a matching spandex. Silver boots hugged her trim ankles, and a dainty silver-gray cowboy hat made more to complement the outfit than for practicality sat cocked saucily on the golden curls, a slim silver cord tightened under her chin to keep it in place.

Tyler tried unsuccessfully to hide his surprise when she answered the door immediately after his knock, already dressed and ready to go at eight o'clock. After a polite but reserved "Morning" he loaded her bags in the Mercedes's trunk and held the car door open for her.

"I hope your room was adequate," he stated coolly as they pulled out of the parking lot and drove through the small downtown section of Sealy. "Of course, it wasn't like the Hilton, where you usually stay, but it was new and clean and the best Sealy has to offer."

Sarah had been biting her tongue to keep from reacting to his barely civil greeting, but this new undeserved assault fired her usually controllable temper.

"What have I done or said to make you treat me so rudely? I haven't acted like a celebrity and don't expect any preferential treatment other than that you provide me with a horse, a place to sleep, and minimal personal protection for the next few days. You've acted like I have some sort of shameful contagious disease that might rub off on you if one kind word escaped your lips. I've got a job to do here, and if we can't come to some sort of terms, then this next week is going to seem a lot longer than just seven days. I've tried my best to be nice and overlook your remarks, but you just keep on and on. . . ." she finished lamely, her large aquamarine eyes shimmering brightly with unshed tears.

"Touché," he responded, then fell silent, a confused frown furrowing his tanned forehead. Several minutes passed before he spoke again, but now his tone was friendlier and more open, as if he had struggled successfully to banish whatever it was that had been troubling him.

"I have to admit that except for the way you dress, you're nothing like what I expected." Unexpectedly he flashed a warm apologetic smile, melting her anger and making her heart skip alarmingly.

"Which was?"

"A bird-witted, fading beauty on a star trip, expecting to be spoonfed and babied, a service I was not eager to provide," he answered ungallantly.

"Try not to sugarcoat it so much." A grin lit up her face. "I can honestly say that that is not me. In fact, I promise you that I'll be out of this business long before I become the creature you described." Only she knew how very true that statement was. By this time next week she would be on her way back home to Kentucky, transformed from a swan back into a duckling. "So can we call a truce and try to get along for the next few days? I've been involved in the music business for years, but I'm very new at this sort of thing and need all the friends I can get, and I don't mean devoted fan-type friends either," she said almost shyly, self-consciously smoothing out nonexistent wrinkles in her form-fitted pants.

A quick glance reassured him that her request was sincere. Impulsively he reached out and covered her small hand with his own much larger one. Although the gesture was meant only to be friendly, Sarah's breath caught in her throat, and she sneaked a look at him from beneath her long lashes, only to catch his own steady gaze fastened on her. This time, however, his eyes weren't the glittery silver that they had been last night but a soft sparkling gray, and they held in their depths an expression suspiciously like admiration, which he quickly masked. Almost guiltily he returned his hand to the steering wheel and his eyes to the road.

After clearing his throat he said, "I don't know if you're as hungry as I am, but if you don't mind waiting a few extra minutes, we can eat a good country-style breakfast at my aunt and uncle's ranch. That's where we're supposed to meet the other trail riders anyway."

"I hate to just drop in on someone and expect them to fix us breakfast," she said hesitantly.

"Well, they are sort of expecting us," he admitted. "They said they would never forgive me if I didn't bring you by to meet them. Aunt Marie probably already has breakfast ready to put on the table."

"It sounds good to me. I'm starved. There's something about getting up early in the morning in the country that increases my appetite alarmingly." She laughed, her naturally cheerful disposition reasserting itself.

When they arrived at the ranch, she demonstrated her hearty appetite by helping herself to generous portions of the delicious breakfast, which included fluffy scrambled eggs, crisp, thick bacon, snowy buttered grits, and flaky buttermilk biscuits still hot from the oven, filled with butter and homemade strawberry preserves.

George and Marie Miller, the middle-aged couple who owned the ranch, hovered around her, watching appreciatively as she ate their food with apparent gusto. They were obviously awed to have seated at their dining-room table a singer who had appeared not once but several times at the Grand Ole Opry. None of their friends or neighbors would ever believe them, so after the meal Marie dug out an old Polaroid camera so they could have their pictures taken with Sarah, who cheerfully obliged, even autographing several record albums they had with Sunny's picture smiling from the covers.

After so many years of handling Sunny's correspondence Sarah could sign Sunny's name better than Sunny herself, but still she couldn't help but feel a twinge of guilt at deceiving this honest, friendly couple who were making her feel so welcome in their home. She had not considered this part of the deception when she had agreed to become Sunny. Everyone who met her this week would, it was to be hoped, assume she was Sunny. But all those people would be victims of a hoax, a fact of which Sarah, with her naturally honest nature, was none too proud. But it was too late now. She was into this too deeply to turn back, so she would just have to concentrate on the benefits of this plan and try not to think about its bad aspects.

Marie adamantly refused Sarah's offer to help with the breakfast dishes and pushed her outside onto the front porch to relax and enjoy the fresh, cool country air. A large weathered wooden swing hung invitingly from one end of the porch that wrapped around the front and one side of the old farmhouse, and Sarah settled comfortably on the bright yellow cushions. Idly she swung back and forth while the men talked ranching, a seemingly endless subject.

This was the life she was meant to lead; she was not really comfortable with the noisy insincerity she had lived with every day for the last seven years. As soon as she got home, she vowed, she would check her savings and investigate the possibility of buying herself a small farm on which to raise horses, cows, chickens, and children . . . not necessarily in that order. Her eyes involuntarily focused on Tyler as he sat on an old cane-back rocker, one powerful leg crossed at the ankle over the other knee, his hat perched on his lap.

He looked incredibly attractive, dressed in a navy blue western shirt and form-fitting jeans that hugged his slim hips and emphasized the well-developed muscles of his long legs. The morning sun glistened on his coal-black hair as it fell carelessly across his broad forehead.

Abruptly Sarah sat up straight, almost upsetting her balance on the swing as she realized with alarm that her train of thought had leapt almost instantaneously from her future and children to Tyler. It was absolutely necessary for her to stop these musings at once. Nothing would complicate this masquerade more than, God forbid, her becoming romantically involved with this man or anyone else she met this week. She must remain detached and keep her cool because there could be no future in any relationship that began while she was pretending to be Sunny.

Shouts and laughter from the approaching trail riders interrupted her thoughts, and she welcomed the intrusion and watched expectantly as hundreds of riders and wagons slowly moved into view. The main body of the group continued to ride by the Millers' ranch without stopping. Only about a dozen riders detached themselves from the impromptu parade to approach the house.

Tyler stood up to greet them, and Sunny followed his lead, gratefully accepting the security his solid presence offered. As if sensing her apprehension, he looked down at her, a small smile warming his eyes. A tingle raced down her spine as his arm circled her slim waist in what she tried to dismiss as a protective gesture. It was probably meant as a display for the nearing riders, but whatever the reason, she was very aware of his nearness, which mysteriously jumbled her normally sensible thoughts. She must remember that this was just a temporary job and accept things at face value without looking for any deeper meanings. There could be none, especially for her.

"Hey, boss," one of the men called, "you been piggin' out on Marie's biscuits again? We had to eat ol' Jed's cooking, and you know what he can do to an egg . . . and it ain't always polite."

"Yeah, some guys have all the luck," another rider snorted good-humoredly. But with that remark all thoughts shifted from food to the delicious-looking morsel at Tyler's side.

"Okay, okay. If you can remember your manners, I'll introduce you to this little lady. You guys had better get it out of your system now, because when we join the

40

others, your job is to take care of Miss Day and look out for her. I don't want to be spending all my time watching you watching her." Tyler's arm tightened possessively. "She's not only a talented singer and mighty easy to look at, but she's turned out to be a real good sport too."

A round of introductions followed, most of which flew over Sarah's head because, for some reason, her mind could only focus on the warm pressure of that muscular arm against her back and the large hand loosely cupping her hipbone. She was reacting like a teenager with her first crush, allowing the slightest touch or hint of a smile to reduce her to a pile of quivering Jell-O.

Sarah was not totally without experience, but she was still a virgin. There had been dozens of men in her life, one of whom she'd been serious enough about to consider marrying, but none had ever held for her this instantaneous, overwhelming attraction that drove coherent thought from her mind and sent goosebumps all over her body. Imagine what would happen to her if he should kiss her! Oh, no, now she was even thinking like a schoolgirl. Impatiently she shook her head to bring herself back to reality and the curious but courteous greetings of the wranglers who surrounded her, their hats in their hands, their eyes showing more interest than their words dared to express.

"That's enough, men. It's time to hit the trail." Tyler brought the unofficial fan club meeting to an abrupt end.

George came from the barn leading two horses. Tyler took the reins of a dainty snow-white mare and handed them to Sarah. "Zena, meet Sunny." He nodded from one to the other solemnly. "Sunny, meet Zena. She's very well mannered and will adapt to your abilities as a rider."

"We'll get along very well, won't we, pretty lady?" Sarah stroked the dished face and small velvety nose of the little Arabian mare. "I've always loved horses, and I'm a very good rider."

"Oh? Have you taken lessons since your famous ride in Iowa?" he asked nonchalantly, his eyes glinting mischievously.

"I didn't . . ." Fiercely she started to defend herself, then paused, silently cursing the position Sunny had put her in. Horseback riding was Sarah's most beloved pastime, and now Sunny's reputation had preceded her to the point that Sarah was again put on the defensive. Well, riding was one thing at which she could shine, and she would enjoy proving herself to this "doubting Tyler."

"As a matter of fact, I took a correspondence course on the plane yesterday. We're having graduation ceremonies next week on the Wonder Horse at Safeway. It's strictly BYOQ, though."

"Okay, I'll bite." The corners of his laughing eyes crinkled as he tried unsuccessfully to look serious. "What's BYOQ?"

"Bring Your Own Quarter," she answered with an impudent wink, then fluidly swung into the saddle unassisted. "Let's go, cowboy. I'm waiting to see Texas—the hard way."

42

Tyler mounted his own large blood-bay gelding and watched skeptically as she handled the mare with the ease and skill of an experienced horsewoman. She was continuing to be full of surprises—all pleasant, so far!

CHAPTER FOUR

By the end of the day it was difficult to tell which part of her body hurt the worst. Grimly she decided it must be either her aching mouth, which had been stretched into what she hoped was a friendly smile for the last six hours, or her bottom, which felt like it had grown to the padded leather saddle seat sometime after lunch.

All in all things had gone better than she had anticipated. Although Sarah was a little out of practice, it had been like stepping back into her childhood to spend a whole day in the saddle with nothing more pressing on her mind than how to keep her hat (and possibly her wig) from being blown off her head by the gusty February wind. Zena was a pure joy with smooth, easy gaits that ate up the miles and the gentle personality that was so characteristic of the Arabian breed.

As expected, the other riders had thronged around Sarah, asking the same old questions she had heard Sunny answer hundreds of times, such as how many gold records did she have and were they really gold, did she write her own songs, and what were Kenny Rogers and Dolly Parton really like? She tried to answer their questions honestly but with the same degree of flippancy that Sunny always used when dealing with the public.

But as the day wore on and most of the riders had had an opportunity to satisfy their curiosity, they began to treat Sarah with polite indifference. Most of them were here to spend a few days escaping from the real world with its pressures and schedules. This was their once-a-year chance to forget tomorrow and have some genuine Texas-style fun.

Sarah could not help but feel a pang of envy at not really belonging to this group of happy-go-lucky people. It wasn't that she wanted more attention because of her "star status." She would have been content just to be one of the riders, accepted for herself and not shown any of the preferential treatment that clearly branded her as an outsider.

The thought pushed into her mind that for this one week she was not down-to-earth Sarah but glow-in-the-dark Sunny, who would never, ever want to be just one of a crowd. It was odd how two people who shared so much could be so different. Except in their taste in men.

Sarah automatically searched for the tall cowboy who was so easy to find among the rest . . . at least for her eyes. There was no doubt in her mind that Sunny, too, would be attracted to this virile, handsome man who without effort could stand out even against a backdrop as majestic as the beautiful countryside through which they were passing. But, then, Sunny was attracted to almost any good-looking male in jeans.

On the other hand, Sarah was always discriminating

and overly cautious about getting involved in any relationship. In fact, she had never met a man who so thoroughly shattered her defenses and stirred her emotions, a fact Tyler was completely unaware of and probably couldn't care less about. Sarah was unsure whether or not his ignorance was fortunate. She should be glad she would not have to worry about his taking advantage of these feelings that were so foreign to her, but then again . . .

"How's our rhinestone cowgirl holding up to the grind?" His deep voice interrupted her thoughts as he pulled his horse alongside hers.

"No problems so far," she fibbed, hoping he would attribute her flushed cheeks to the breeze. "You and your men have done a good job of handling my fans. Most of them are really terrific, but a few came on a little strong."

"Wait until around midnight, after they've gotten a few more six packs under their belts," he warned. "Things sometimes get a little rowdy."

"I hope to be fast asleep long before then." She shifted slightly in the saddle, searching for a more comfortable position.

His perceptive gaze took in her movement, and he said with a twinkle, "We're almost to the camp. Jed should have dinner about ready. It gets dark early this time of year, and most of these people will hit the sack soon after they eat tonight. The first two days on the trail always seem to be the hardest on urban cowboys."

"Saddles do take a certain amount of reacquaintance," she admitted, her full lips curving into a grin. "Horseback riding is like bicycle riding: You never really forget how to do it, but the end result can be a little painful until your muscles cooperate."

He laughed, a rich, deep rumble that enveloped her warmly. She was glad when he made no move to ride away but stayed at her side for the rest of the day's journey. All day he had never been far from her, always within sight in case she needed him, but, then, that was part of his job. She reminded herself not to read too much into his nearness, but still she was happier now that he was beside her.

A parking lot of pickup trucks, vans, and campers in assorted sizes awaited the weary trail riders. Although the riders enjoyed the "back to basics" feel of spending long hours in the saddle, most welcomed the luxury of a semisoft bed in a dry, warm camper. It was difficult for these modern-day pioneers to give up all the conveniences they were accustomed to, such as televisions, radios, and running water. There were some, however, who stubbornly refused comfort and insisted on roughing it all the way by spreading sleeping bags on the ground or bunking in the covered wagons that accompanied the trail riders.

Sarah didn't know what to expect as far as her sleeping arrangements were concerned, but again Tyler had done his job well. As they rode into camp he led her to what appeared to be a small mobile home. After dismounting he walked around to her horse and held up his hands to help her down. Gingerly she threw her leg over the saddlehorn and slid out of the saddle into his waiting arms, trying to ignore the thrill that raced through her body at his touch. Handling her carefully so that their bodies didn't meet, he released her as soon as her boots hit the ground and turned abruptly toward the camper.

"Here's where you'll be staying," he said as he unlocked the door and pulled down the front step. "It's not the—"

"I know, I know. It's not the Hilton," she teased as she stepped inside and looked around her in awe. It was truly a little home on wheels, and much plusher than she would ever have imagined. They were standing in a small living/dining area with what appeared to be a compact but well-equipped kitchen to the left. Thick padded carpet covered all the floors and was the same muted shade of blue as the striped wallpaper.

"The bedroom and bathroom are to the right. There should be plenty of hot water and towels. Help yourself to everything here and let me know if there's anything else you need." He gestured as he spoke, never leaving the trailer's open doorway. "That control over there on the wall is for the heater. The kitchen is fairly well stocked, but Jed is an excellent cook in spite of what my men said earlier, and he provides us with all of our meals. You'll find your luggage in the bedroom."

"It's really very nice," Sarah commented.

"Well, I hope you'll be comfortable here for the next few days."

"I'm sure I will be. I know you probably won't believe me, but I've stayed in many hotels that were a lot worse

48

than this. And you know something else?" She grinned mischievously. "I've never stayed at a Hilton."

"Give me a break," he moaned. "I won't ever accuse you of high living again. I hope you won't be spoiled by staying here. Perhaps you'd rather sleep in the back of a pickup truck?" he suggested devilishly.

"Oh, no. I'll force myself to be comfortable here."

"I'll check in on you later." He chuckled. "But I've got some tired horses that need my attention now."

It was already dark when she finished her shower. She felt much better but decided it was too much of an effort to get completely redressed. Sunny's idea of nightwear for a trail ride probably bore no resemblance to anything that any of the other women would be wearing to bed, but Sarah had brought nothing of her own and had to make do with what had been packed.

The negligee was made of an antique white satin with deep ruffles of delicate lace around the plunging V neck and long full sleeves. The gown itself smoothly followed the curves of her body, but the robe was fuller and belted at the waist by a wide satin ribbon. It was really very becoming against her lightly tanned skin, but not exactly what Sarah would have chosen to wear camping out in a trailer.

Since she didn't plan to put in any more appearances tonight, she also didn't see any need to put that hateful wig back on and left her hair piled up on her head, held loosely in place by several enameled combs. Tiny golden tendrils escaped to curl around her cheeks and neck. Her face felt pounds lighter with Sunny's heavy makeup replaced by only a touch of mascara and a dash of lip gloss. Thank goodness she had already done her daily interview for the Houston television stations that were covering this trail ride, so no more performances would be expected of her today. Even Jed's cooking would have to wait until tomorrow, because she had no intention of leaving this trailer tonight.

As she was rummaging through the kitchen, trying to decide what to fix for herself, someone knocked at the door. Sarah considered pretending not to hear, but her visitor was persistent and knocked again. Swearing under her breath, she called, "Who's there?"

"It's me, Tyler. Are you okay?"

"Yes, I'm fine. I already took a shower and was getting ready to fix something for dinner."

"Jed's got everything ready, and he made enough for Sam Houston's army."

"I wasn't planning to go out again tonight."

"Do you think you could open the door? I really feel stupid hollering like this."

Sarah felt a moment's panic as her hand flew to her untidy hair. She was not exactly dressed to receive visitors, but it would be very rude to keep him shouting through her closed door. Besides, she thought, Tyler had already seen much more of the "real her" than she would have liked, and it was a little late to be bashful now. If only she could stall him for a few minutes so she could comb her hair . . . but what did it really matter? With a sigh she opened the door and greeted him with a smile.

"Uh . . ." He stared at her blankly. She couldn't possibly be aware of how bewitching she looked at that moment with her tousled hair glowing in the artificial light and her body clearly outlined through her thin clothing. He tried to tell himself that she had planned it this way, but there was an honest innocence in her expression that convinced him otherwise. "Did I interrupt anything?" he asked, somewhat suspiciously.

"No, I was just looking for something simple to cook. The shower revived me, but I just couldn't face any more interviews today."

"I'll go get you a plate," he offered, anxious to leave before he made any other offers that would embarrass them both.

"Are you sure it wouldn't be any trouble?" she asked, forgetting that Sunny would never have thought of such a question, but fortunately Tyler's mind was on something else.

"Not at all. It's part of my job to see that you're well fed."

"Okay, but only if you agree to bring yourself back a plate, too, and eat here with me." She surprised herself with the suggestion but was glad she had because suddenly the idea of eating by herself in a strange trailer made her feel lonely.

Tyler seemed even more shocked at the suggestion and was momentarily speechless. He wasn't sure he could make it through a meal with her dressed like that and retain his professionalism. His mind searched for an acceptable excuse for refusing, but he came up with nothing. "I guess that would be all right. I'll be back in a minute," he finally managed to reply.

After he left, Sarah tried to decide whether or not she should change her clothes and fix her hair. She didn't want to draw attention to herself by appearing to dress up for him, but she didn't want him to get the wrong impression about her either. Her clothing was a little suggestive, but it wasn't transparent, and it covered her from neck to foot. And he had already seen her like this, so it would look obvious if she changed her clothes or rearranged her hair. What difference would it make? she chided herself. He had certainly never shown any personal interest in her, and even if he did, there was nothing she could do about it. So, instead of redressing, she returned to the kitchen and began setting the table.

He reappeared carrying a tray loaded with enough food for a family of four and a pitcher of iced tea. Sarah closed the door behind him, then followed him to the table.

"There's some good plates in the cabinet," he commented when he saw the paper plates she had found.

"These are fine with me. I'm not overly fond of washing dishes, but if you would prefer the others . . ." she began.

"I eat on paper plates all the time," he admitted. "But you—"

"Oh, darn," she said with a grin. "The Reagans gave me a place setting of their White House china that I use for everyday meals, but I forgot to pack it."

"I can't figure you out," he said honestly. "You're so—"

"Hungry," she supplied. "Quit talking, and let's eat, cowboy."

That crooked grin she was becoming so familiar with spread across his face as he sat down. Without further delay they attacked the food, savoring each tender bite of T-bone steak and stuffed baked potato. There was a crisp green salad and hot yeast rolls, dripping with butter, with fresh peach cobbler for dessert.

"How can he cook that well on an open fire?" she asked as she pushed back from the table.

"Years of practice." He glanced at his watch. "It's getting pretty late. You wanted to get to bed early tonight, didn't you?"

She stood up and started clearing the table. "I'll just wash these glasses and silverware. Thanks for bringing the meal. I don't believe I could have thrown together anything even half as good."

"You cook too?" he asked.

"Don't sound so shocked. I don't get much practice, but my mother must be one of the best cooks in Kentucky, and I picked up a few things from her."

"That's good to know in case Jed gets sick," he teased.

"In that case, let's hope for his continued good health . . . and ours," she answered as she squirted dishwashing detergent into the water. Pushing the lacy sleeves up past her elbows, she plunged her hands into the soapy water, then looked up in surprise as Tyler joined her at the sink.

"What are you doing?" she asked as he unbuttoned his cuffs and rolled them up.

"I guess if Sunny Day, superstar and singing sensation of the eighties, can wash dishes, I can too," he joked.

"There's not that many."

"Then we'll finish twice as fast," he reasoned.

But his nearness caused her fingers to tremble so badly, she wasn't sure it was wise for her to be handling the sharp steak knives. As she dropped the forks into the rinse water on his side of the sink and he reached for them, their hands met. For just an instant Tyler and Sarah froze, the current passing back and forth between them. She raised her eyes to his and was startled by the smoldering passion that momentarily darkened them to a stormy gray. Nervously the pink tip of her tongue darted out to moisten her lips, but when she noticed his eyes following its movement, she clamped her mouth shut and dropped her gaze.

Almost reluctantly he pulled his hand away and reached for the forks. Showing his discomfort, he cleared his throat before stating in a husky voice, "It's really a shame that we can't spend more time here in San Felipe."

"Why?" she asked, wanting him to say because he wanted to be here alone with her.

"Because no one should ever pass through this town without seeing some of the sights."

"Oh, really?" She tried to hide her disappointment.

"This place is one of the oldest and most historical spots in all of Texas," he rattled on to fill the heavy silence. "San Felipe's population today is probably less than five hundred, but before Texas won its battle for independence from Mexico in 1836, this little town was the place to be."

Under different circumstances Sarah would have found this information very interesting, but right now she was hearing more than she really wanted to know about this place. Why couldn't Tyler shut up and kiss her? Her whole body throbbed with that thought as she reacted to the proximity of his imposing masculinity. Never had the trailer seemed so small as it did when his broad shoulders filled the room. She loved the faint lingering scent of his spicy after-shave, mixed with the pleasing odor of horses and his own personal smell. The combination was like an aphrodisiac that left her feeling slightly dizzy and longing for something her common sense told her she could never have.

"San Felipe has the distinction of having had the first post office, the first English school, and the first official Sunday school in Texas. The whole town was burned to the ground by Texans who didn't want to leave anything behind for Santa Anna's troops, but many of the buildings were rebuilt and are still in use today," he finished, once again in control of himself.

He had come close before, much too close for his own peace of mind, to making a complete fool of himself. This woman had powers he was totally unprepared to resist. He had never expected this aura of innocence, vulnerability, and total femininity that surrounded her. It taunted him, firing his passion to a fever pitch that was increasingly difficult to deny. With her beauty, her talent, and her surprisingly unassuming charm, he was sure she had more offers than she could handle.

Tyler had not wanted to be responsible for this prima donna, but as he was chairman of the Trail Ride Committee, the duty had fallen naturally to him, and he had vowed he would make the best of the situation. But never had he guessed his detachment would prove to be so difficult to maintain.

"How did you know?" she asked conversationally.

"Know what?" His mind searched frantically, but he was having difficulty forming coherent thoughts.

"How did you know all of that information about San Felipe?"

"Oh, that." He sighed, relieved that she hadn't been able to read his disturbing thoughts. "I was a history buff in school. When I first started on this trail ride and found out it roughly followed the Texas Independence Trail, I did a little research on the places we pass through."

"I never was that good at history. Maybe you could point some of these places out for me as we go along," she suggested, hopeful that this new duty would keep him closer to her side—although that could prove to be a mixed blessing if she couldn't smother these wild desires she was experiencing.

"If you're sure you wouldn't be bored, I'd be glad to." He was pleased by her interest and the prospect of spending more time with her.

She had never felt less bored in her life. "Maybe you can succeed where Mr. Armstrong failed."

"Mr. Armstrong?"

"My high school history teacher. He gave up on me somewhere between the Spanish-American War and the Civil War."

"The Civil War came first," he said, correcting her automatically.

"See? He was right." She smiled, daring another glance at his attractive face.

The sparkle in her eyes and her endearing smile proved too much for him, and he decided it was time to beat a hasty retreat before it became impossible for him to leave her tonight.

"Reveille will come awful early tomorrow morning, and even though you don't need any more beauty sleep, I do," he said quickly, and left before she even realized his intention.

It was with a mixture of regret and relief that she locked the door behind him. Sunny would never know the sacrifice this masquerade was costing Sarah. She had probably met the one perfect man that had been allotted to her during her lifetime, and he didn't know her as herself but as her sister. How had things gotten so complicated and out of control in such a short time? With a heartfelt sigh Sarah let exhaustion overtake her as she crawled into the roomy queen-size bed and slept.

CHAPTER FIVE

She thought he had been joking, but sure enough, just after dawn the next day, a recorded version of reveille blared over a loudspeaker, effectively rousing the sleeping trail riders. Groans and good-natured grumblings were heard as a slightly subdued group made their individual preparations for the new day.

Sarah stifled a yawn as she left the trailer and headed toward the tantalizing breakfast smells of brewing coffee and fresh biscuits that wafted to her in the still morning air. She thrust her hands deep into the narrow pockets of her tight jeans, hunching her shoulders to ward off the slight chill. It was another beautiful cloudless day. Although there was a little nip in the air, Sarah knew that once the sun rose higher in the sky, the temperature would be in the high sixties, so she didn't bother with a jacket.

Tyler separated from the crowd and strode toward her, carrying two steaming mugs of hot coffee. Thanking him, she took one, cupping her hands around its warmth while taking small eye-opening sips.

"I hope you like it strong. I don't think Jed knows how

to make it any other way," Tyler commented, his gray eyes taking in every detail of her trim form, dressed today in a bright lemon-yellow silk blouse, decorated with a white fringe and tiny white seed pearls. Her wig was properly in place and the makeup dramatically applied, but he no longer saw those artificial adornments, because he had gotten an all too brief glimpse of the natural woman beneath them.

"I can drink anyone's coffee. Over the years I've developed a cast-iron stomach." She smiled at him through the rising steam. "It's other parts of my body that I'm more concerned about."

"So we're a little sore today, are we?" he asked.

"I don't know about you, but I couldn't get my knees to touch each other this morning. I'll bet I'm two inches shorter than I was yesterday because my legs simply refuse to straighten. I had to lie on the bed to get my jeans on," she added. "But, then, if she had bought them one size larger, I might be able to bend normally."

"She who?"

"My . . . uh, sister," Sarah stammered. "She bought all of these clothes for me to take on this trip."

"Just think of all the little silkworms and oysters that worked overtime for that one blouse," he quipped as he reached out and flicked the fringe that dangled from her cuff.

"Yes, we do our best to keep the sequin and rhinestone factories in business." She tore her gaze away from his rugged face and stared into the dark liquid in her mug.

"What can I get you for breakfast? Jed's got biscuits, bacon, sausage, and scrambled eggs," he offered.

"I'll just have a biscuit and a sausage, please. I'm still full from last night's meal," she answered. Her unconsciously wistful blue gaze followed his tall, lithe body as he returned to the fire. She had never really appreciated the triangular symmetry of the male form before, but, then, none of the male forms she had seen could even begin to compare with Tyler's. There was just something about this man that charged all five of her senses with the unbridled intensity of an electrical storm. Even her skin seemed to tingle when he was near. She should have the good sense to be frightened of these curiously pleasant sensations, but instead she longed to venture deeper into the tempest and experience its full promise. Sunny would —without hesitation. But she wasn't Sunny.

"Miss Day"—a young man holding a clipboard walked up to her and held out his hand—"I'm Bob Thompson, the program director for *Good Morning Houston,* and we have our camera crews here today and were hoping that you would consent to doing an interview."

It was a timely reminder that she *was* Sunny, at least for the next few days. But should the charade continue into the night with a man who would never know the real truth?

"Miss Day?" Bob tried again.

"Oh, yes. I'm sorry," she apologized, rewarding his diligence with a dazzling smile. "Of course, I would love to be on your show. Am I dressed properly for your cameras, or should I change?"

60

"You look perfect just the way you are. In fact, all the photographs I've seen of you don't do you justice," he went on effusively. "If you'll follow me, I'll introduce you to Jan Glenn and Don Nelson, the hosts of *Good Morning Houston.* I'm sure they'll be just as thrilled to meet you as I am."

Tyler had returned with her breakfast and was waiting somewhat impatiently, a dark scowl on his handsome face. As Bob jotted a quick note on his clipboard Sarah shrugged and tried to tell Tyler with her eyes that it was just another part of the game and for him not to take it personally. She hoped she had gotten the message across, because Bob propelled her across to a van that had a large *13* and *Eyewitness News* painted on its sides and an antenna mounted on its top.

Both hosts were very warm and friendly, immediately putting Sarah at ease. She wasn't used to being interviewed, but she'd seen Sunny handle it so many times that she knew she could pull it off. After the cameras had been set up and an impromptu stage arranged in front of one of the covered wagons, the interview began with the hosts confessing that they were fans of hers and delighted to meet her.

"Are you enjoying the trail ride, Sunny?" Jan asked. "I have to admit that I don't think I could make it for a whole week. I ride in the parade every year and enjoy it, but this would be just a little too much of a good thing."

"I'm having a terrific time. It's been so long since I've been able to spend time outdoors, breathing this fresh, clean country air and enjoying the scenery," Sarah answered honestly. "And even though I perform in front of thousands of people each year, I never have the opportunity to meet many of my fans. I think some degree of personal contact is important for a performer to keep her perspective."

"You perform on the road quite a lot, don't you?"

"Yes, usually about three hundred days out of the year, which gets grueling for even the most seasoned performer," Sarah admitted.

"I can imagine," Jan sympathized.

"Of course, it does have its rewards. It pays well as long as the tickets keep selling. And touring helps to boost record sales. Also it fulfills that certain something deep within me that prompted me to walk up on a stage for the first time and sing my heart out to anyone who cared to listen. Back then it didn't matter whether or not they paid me—I just wanted to perform in front of an audience."

"I've noticed that performers do seem to be driven by some invisible force. I don't think they would be content to live their lives without that opportunity for self-expression, do you?" Jan asked perceptively.

"You're absolutely right. I don't understand it myself, but performing can be as vital to a person's survival as eating and breathing," Sarah agreed, thinking of Sunny. Even when she was on the verge of exhaustion, she still pushed herself, traveling to one more concert so she could get out there and do what she did best: sing.

The cameraman motioned that they had to cut to a commercial, and everyone took advantage of the break to drink their coffee or have their hair retouched. Sarah stayed where she was, but when she looked up, she saw Tyler standing behind one of the cameramen. He was studying her with an oddly intimate look that made her heart lurch. It took all her self-control not to rush over to him and throw herself into his arms. But as quickly as his look had appeared, it was replaced by a detached impersonal one that made her wonder if she had read too much into his expression.

The camera light blinked back on, and the interview continued from the point where they had left off earlier.

"Now let's get a little more personal," Jan said with a conspiratorial smile. "With all of this traveling how do you have time for any sort of meaningful relationships?"

To Sarah's dismay she could feel a light blush staining her cheeks. This was a subject better left undiscussed with her own feelings in such a turmoil.

"Is there someone special in your life right now?" Jan pried gently.

"Do I look like the type to kiss and tell?" Sarah responded evasively with a saucy toss of her blond curls.

Jan leaned forward slightly and prompted, "Your romantic involvements have gotten quite a lot of press coverage. I thought you might like to have the opportunity to set the record straight once and for all."

"For most of my life my energy has been focused on developing a successful career," Sarah said thoughtfully. Perhaps this was a chance to help her sister's credibility by sweeping away some of the half-truths and emphasizing her dedication. "I admit that I do attend my share of parties, but if I was half as wild and wicked as has been reported, I wouldn't have the strength or stamina to keep to my tough schedule.

"And as far as a serious relationship goes, it would take a very special man to understand and tolerate my situation." How true that statement was, she thought to herself. If only Tyler could be open-minded enough to accept her as Sarah and not be disappointed and disgusted by her deception.

The interview changed course, and for the next few minutes they discussed Sunny's music and future plans. Jan and Don said they looked forward to seeing her at the parade in Houston on Saturday. After the interview Bob promised to save her a video tape of the show, which had been aired live.

Tyler was no longer standing where she had seen him last, so Sarah headed for her trailer. She was almost at the door when she saw him walking toward her, leading his gelding.

"Where's Zena? She's not hurt, is she?" Sarah's voice was filled with concern.

"No, she's fine," he answered, peering at her inquisitively. "I didn't know whether you were planning on riding her or the front seat of a pickup truck today."

"I thought we had discussed this last night. Of course I want to ride Zena. This is a trail ride. I didn't fly all the way to Houston to sit in a pickup truck," she retorted, frustrated by the sudden change in his attitude toward her. It appeared that Tyler was trying to avoid her company. Apparently he hadn't been looking forward to

64

today's ride as much as she had. Which was just as well, she tried to reassure herself, because the attraction was too strong, and she needed to remember how dangerous an involvement would be.

"But I don't want you to feel like you have to ride with me. I'm sure one of your men would be happy to take your place if you have other more pressing duties," she purred sarcastically.

For several seconds they glared at each other, their pride and uncertainty looming between them like a brick wall.

"You're the boss," he sneered. "I'll get someone to saddle Zena and bring her over here." And he turned on his heel, mounted his horse, and left her standing on the step, too furious to call him back for the explanation she felt she deserved.

When her new escort arrived with Zena, Sarah knew Tyler was getting the last laugh. Thank goodness she, too, had a good sense of humor, for this new turn of events would surely have tested the patience of a saint.

The man, who probably would never see seventy again, looked like he had just ridden out of a rerun of *Gunsmoke.* He was dressed in baggy well-worn denim overalls that had faded to a soft bluish white after many washings and which succeeded in making his thin figure appear even more gaunt. A red plaid flannel shirt peeked out from beneath a canvas coat that must be at least two sizes too large.

"You ready to hit the trail, Miss Sunny?" he asked

before turning to spit a dark stream of tobacco juice away from her.

"Sure thing," she answered, refusing to be intimidated by this ancient specimen. He started to get down to help her mount, but she was already settled on Zena before he had even swung his right leg over the back of his saddle. As she urged the beautifully dainty mare forward Sarah decided that possibly the most disconcerting thing about the man was the animal on which he sat.

It was, without a doubt, the ugliest mule Sarah had ever seen. Tall and gangly, its coat the color of wet bark, the animal flipped its long lop ears backward, waiting for its master's command. It was an old joke that owners and their animals began to resemble each other after long years of association, and Sarah had never seen a case that confirmed this axiom more than this odd couple.

Silently they fell in with the others as they left the camp behind. Sarah was trying to think of a subject they could possibly have in common when he spoke again.

"My name's Willie. In my younger days folks called me Wild Willie, but nowadays they call me Weird Willie." He cackled gleefully.

Sarah looked at him doubtfully. Surely Tyler wouldn't send her an escort that wasn't playing with a full deck. She met Willie's very pale blue eyes and saw, not insanity but a sharpness undimmed by age. This little old man was playing a joke on the world and enjoying it immensely.

"Ty told me you're interested in soaking in some local color as we go. Ain't no one better equipped to do that

66

than ol' Willie here, 'cause I've been riding on this trail ride every year since it started back in 1952. Yep, me and Ethyl never miss one," he added, directing another stream of juice over his shoulder.

"Who's Ethyl?" Sarah was impelled to ask, wondering if an equally old and strange lady was somewhere among the long line of trail riders.

"Ethyl's my mule," he explained as he bent down and patted the shaggy neck, sending up a cloud of dust.

"Why did you name her Ethyl?" she queried, wondering if perhaps it was the name of an old flame or his mother.

" 'Cause it ain't regular!" Willie hooted, delighted that he had suckered her into his favorite joke.

"Oh, no." Sarah groaned at the corn pone humor. She would pay Tyler back for this if it took the rest of her life. Frantically she tried to change the subject.

"Do you live in Houston, Willie?"

"Nope. You won't catch me in no city. There's just too many people all jammed together, fighting the traffic and cussin' their neighbors. That's what's wrong with the United States today."

When he didn't expand on this statement, Sarah was prompted to ask, "What's wrong with the United States?"

"I'll tell you." He nodded wisely. "There's more people than cattle. Nineteen eighty-one was the first year in Texas's history when the humans outnumbered the cattle, and as far as I'm concerned, that was the beginning of the end."

"Surely it can't be that disastrous," Sarah said, trying to placate him.

"Just think about all the places that have given us taxes, crime, and politics and tell me what the human/cattle ratio is. There's something honest and dependable about a cow. Some of my best friends are cows."

"Does Ethyl know?" she asked in a theatrical whisper which drew his pleased guffaw.

"Ty told me you weren't half-bad."

"Which means I'm not half-good," she muttered under her breath.

"What's that?" Willie leaned closer so he could hear her.

"It's a personal joke," she said louder, then added, "And I have a few things I'd like to tell Tyler right now."

"Hey, go easy on ol' Ty. He's been acting real strange lately. I think he's upset about something or other."

"Do you know him well?" At last there was a subject she was vitally interested in discussing.

"As well as anyone, I guess. He sort of keeps to himself. But his grandfather and me go way back."

Questions flew through her mind, and she wondered if it would be possible to satisfy her curiosity without seeming obvious. Throwing caution to the wind, she queried casually, "Was his father a rancher too?"

"Yep, and his grandfather before that. They have a pretty sizable spread down south of Houston near a little town called Alvin. Used to run a few hundred head of cattle on it, but now they mostly just raise rodeo stock and longhorns."

Sarah's thoughts sped ahead to the days when she would have her own farm and would have to decide what type of livestock she could raise and enjoy while still making ends meet. "You mean they can make a living raising pleasure animals?"

"Yeah, that and a few dozen oil and gas wells that have been drilled on their land." He spat again and added in a disgusted tone, "If you ask me, those dang machines sure take away from the beauty of a piece of land."

"Not too many people would agree with you on that score."

"That'd be nothin' new," he said with a snort. "Not too many people agree with me about anything."

"Does anyone live on the ranch with Tyler?" she began, then hastily added, "I mean, are his parents still alive?"

Willie slid her a knowing glance and said, "Ty's dad died several years back, but his mother still lives there at the ranch house. She's a real fine woman. Ty's a lot like her. They're just good, honest, hard-workin' folks."

"Is there anyone else living there?" she persisted, wondering if perhaps Tyler had been cool toward her because he was engaged or even married. A cold chill chased through her as she realized that she didn't even know that simple fact about him. She didn't pause to ask herself why it mattered so much when she knew that regardless of his personal situation there could never be anything permanent between the two of them. But it did matter—a great deal. "Any brothers or sisters maybe?"

"Nope, just the two of them. Ty's mother's been after

him for years to find a good woman and settle down, but he just laughs and tells her that he's looking for someone just like her but hasn't hit it lucky yet."

Sarah fell into a depressed silence. So Tyler was looking for a good, honest, hard-working woman just like his mother? She might have come close to fitting that description last week, but just look at her now. Whatever relationship they might be able to build would be based on a lie. The initial relief she had felt when she had discovered he wasn't married fled in the face of this glaring problem. The only truth in this whole situation was that she was interested in a man who might or might not be interested in the person he thought was her sister.

If only there were some way she could discover why he was so inconsistent. Just when she thought she could trust him, he would switch moods, leaving her baffled. Perhaps she could think of a way to gauge his reaction to her participation in this deception before she made a complete fool of herself; and more importantly, before she did anything that could damage Sunny's career.

It was imperative that she not lose sight of her original mission because of the uncharacteristic emotional chaos that engulfed her. Sunny was depending on her, and she couldn't ruin it now just because of a strong physical attraction to a man who never acted the same way twice.

"No, wait a minute," Willie burst into her thoughts. "Ty was engaged a few years ago to a girl he had gone to school with. But there was some sort of commotion about a baby and her career, and then they busted up." His voice trailed off thoughtfully.

The old man had effectively captured Sarah's undivided attention. "What sort of commotion?" she prompted gently.

"It was right after his dad died that this girl Ty had dated all through college came up in a family way. Well, Ty being the kind of guy he is, he right away offered to marry her." Willie reached into his overalls pocket for a fresh plug of tobacco while Sarah waited impatiently for him to continue.

"She was a real looker. I remember that they made a right smart-looking pair, but then some guy from New York offered her a modeling job in Europe. She told Ty some cock-and-bull story about visiting her sick old aunt because she knew he wouldn't like the idea of her prancing around half-dressed one bit.

"But he found out about her little job and that she had gotten rid of the baby so she wouldn't ruin her figure. I haven't ever seen him so fightin' mad. Well, when she came back, expecting to go on with the wedding and telling him a lie about how she had suffered a miscarriage at her aunt's, he came all unglued. Turned out it wasn't even his baby, but of course she didn't tell him that until after he'd thrown her out. Since then he's been real cautious when it comes to women. She hurt him real bad, and now he don't trust any of 'em at all, and he don't abide with no lying."

Sarah had listened to the story in shocked silence. She understood Tyler's pain and sympathized with him, but he shouldn't judge all women by this one bad experience. She was sure this must have something to do with his

71

moodiness. Although she wouldn't be able to talk with him about it, perhaps later she could think of some way to make him see that not all women were dishonest and deceptive. With a jolt she realized that she was a poor one to be trying to convince Tyler of anything. He must never learn of her own lies or he would hate her for her hypocrisy. Frantically she pushed thoughts of Tyler from her mind.

"So, tell me, Willie, how has the Salt Grass Trail Ride changed over the years?" She knew she could depend on him to get her mind back to a safer subject, even if she couldn't always follow his confusing train of thought. "How did it all start in the first place?"

"Well, the way I understand it, the folks who put on the Houston fat stock show were trying to find a way to get people interested in their yearly shindig. A friend of mine worked for one of the local TV stations and came up with the idea of getting some cowboys to drive a covered wagon into Houston from some little country town.

"There were four of us on that first trail ride, and I ain't never had such a good time since. We just took our time, making like we was back in the olden days. Course we had to keep in touch 'cause they were using us for publicity. And it worked real good, 'cause from then on folks couldn't wait for the chance to play cowboy once a year."

"Did you travel along this same route?" Sarah asked, beginning to be fascinated by this colorful old man.

"Not really. We started from Brenham that year. We made it look like so much fun that now there are at least a dozen other trail rides. The Old Spanish Trail Ride starts from some place in Louisiana and is over twice as long as ours. And there's even one with a Spanish name, Los Vaqueros Rio Grande, that leaves Hidalgo, near the Texas-Mexico border. It lasts almost two weeks and covers just under four hundred miles," Willie explained. Most of the people on this trail ride already knew all of this information, and he welcomed the opportunity to show off his knowledge to such an attractive and interested audience.

"I never realized these things were so popular. This must be one of the most successful promotional gimmicks in the history of rodeos," Sarah commented.

"Even though it's February and the weather's usually cold enough to freeze the horns off a billy goat, there's still over six thousand tenderfoot cowboys a year dragging into Houston on all these trail rides. If they held this thing in the summertime, there'd be at least twice that many riders. So I guess you could say it has attracted some interest." He prodded Ethyl with his heels as the mule tried to grab a mouthful of dry grass. "The Salt Grass Trail Ride may not be the longest, but we're the oldest and biggest," he added proudly.

"I'll bet you and Ethyl have enough stories to make an interesting book. You probably know more about the history of the Salt Grass Trail Ride than anyone else. Did you ever keep any sort of journal or diary?"

"I ain't much good at puttin' things down on paper, and old Ethyl's memory ain't what it used to be. I just like to pass on my stories to those folks that want to hear them. But nowadays most folks just don't have the time to listen to the past."

Sarah was deeply touched. It must be sad to grow old in a world that moved too fast to care about a lonely old man and his memories. She looked at him with a new perspective, and the next four hours passed quickly as he eagerly shared with her some memories of his life. She became so engrossed that she temporarily forgot her sister, her problems, and the tall black-haired cowboy who, unbeknownst to her, had never let her out of his sight all day.

CHAPTER SIX

They set up camp that night just outside of Brookshire. That day's ride had been the shortest leg of the trip; it was planned that way to give everyone time to get the kinks out and become accustomed to the routine.

Although Sarah's soreness had been worked out, she couldn't shake the feeling that she was walking bowlegged as she left Zena with one of the cowboys and waved to Willie. He was really a nice old man, and she had enjoyed herself. She would have enjoyed herself a lot more if a certain someone hadn't been so aloof, but she had more pride than to ask him to ride with her if he felt he had to force himself to tolerate her company.

"Uh, excuse me, Miss Day."

Sarah stopped as a young man she recognized as one of Tyler's cowboys stepped in front of her. "Yes?" Her golden brown eyebrows arched expectantly.

"A group of us were going into town tonight for dinner and a few drinks. Brookshire has this restaurant named the Cotton Gin that used to be a—"

"Let me guess," she interrupted with a friendly smile. "I'll bet it was a cotton gin, right?"

"Right!" He grinned back at her, encouraged. "But it really does have good food, and we thought you might want to come along with us. Oh, but you don't have to worry about being mobbed or anything. There will be a big group from the trail ride there, and we all stick together," he hastened to add.

She looked at his appealing face with adoration clearly written across it. Possibly a night on the town, however small the town might be, was just the therapy she needed. She had no doubt that Sunny would not pass up an opportunity to party, but Sarah's heart just wasn't in it.

"Thanks for asking me, but I think I'll pass. You guys go on and have a good time," she answered. Then at his crestfallen look she added, "Maybe next time."

"Yeah, sure." He was obviously disappointed. It would have been the highlight of his young life to hang out with *the* Sunny Day. Maybe after a few drinks she would have forgotten he was a nobody and . . . Well, there was no use in dreaming about something that would never happen. "See you tomorrow, then."

"Good night." She left him and hurried to her trailer for a much needed shower. She would have preferred a deep tub filled with fragrant bubble bath in which she could immerse her tired body for the next hour. But the bathroom in the trailer was barely large enough for a corner tub that was too small for her even to sit in and straighten her legs. It wasn't worth the effort, so she took advantage of the hot shower.

Properly revived and smelling like a lady again, she dressed in a ruby red satin jump suit that showed off her

76

shapely figure to perfection. She had to work for several minutes on the windblown wig, but after a reapplication of makeup she stared at a very creditable image of Sunny Day in all her glory.

This was Tuesday night. That meant there were only three days left of her once-in-a-lifetime chance to be someone special. But all the gushy attention was beginning to get on her nerves, and she certainly wouldn't miss the glittery clothes and wig. Regardless of what Sunny had said, Sarah would never feel completely comfortable in this getup.

She had lived on the fringe of the glamor for too long not to be able to see through the falseness. People loved or hated Sunny for what they thought she was, but few of them cared enough to look beneath the surface. Sarah would be glad to return to being her untalented, unexciting self, except for one confusing, unforgettable reason. She knew that when she left Texas next Sunday, she would be leaving behind more than she had bargained for.

Her stomach growled, reminding her that she had missed breakfast and only picked at her lunch. Surely Jed would have something delicious cooked for supper. She didn't want to spend an evening alone in this trailer. Not after last night, when Tyler's presence had seemed to fill and brighten every dark corner. He had probably gone into town with the others. Of course he would have left some men behind to take care of her, and maybe they wouldn't mind if she joined them.

There was quite a crowd around Jed, some helping and

some just getting in the way as he tried to prepare supper. A huge friendly bonfire crackled and beckoned Sarah to its warmth. Almost shyly she joined the group, most of whom she recognized but didn't really know. But they greeted her with friendly smiles, and one of the men got up so she could have a campstool on which to sit.

By the end of the meal she no longer felt like an outsider. It was wonderful to be accepted at last; able to join in normal conversations with people who realized she had more to talk about than gold records and Grammy Awards. Someone brought out an ice chest full of cold beer and wine, which was quickly distributed and consumed.

Sarah sipped at her glass of wine, enjoying the stories and jokes that were becoming increasingly ribald as the evening progressed. Occasionally she joined in, but mostly she just listened, watching the fire and wondering what Tyler was doing right now.

"What are you doing here?" His unexpected voice nearly caused her to choke on her wine.

"Where am I supposed to be?"

He found an empty stool and pulled it up next to hers, lowering his voice so as not to disturb the others' conversation. "I checked your trailer. You weren't there, of course, so I assumed you had gone into town with the others. They did ask you, didn't they?"

"Yes, they did, but I have been known to pass up a party. I thought it would be more fun to hang around here, and I'm glad I did." She resented him for immediately putting her on the defensive. "Why didn't you go

78

with them? I thought you might need the night off from your bothersome job."

A muscle in his strong square jaw was working overtime as he leaned closer to hiss in her ear, "You know I don't still feel that way about you."

"Well, that's news to me. You avoided me like the plague today and pawned me off on poor Willie like I was a pair of hand-me-down shoes," she whispered back petulantly.

"You two seemed to get along okay." Grudging admiration warmed his voice. "He was quite overwhelmed by you, and that's some compliment. He doesn't take to many people."

"You were lucky we finally hit it off. For a while there I was thinking of creative ways of paying you back."

"If you wanted me to get someone else to ride with you, you should have just said so," he said with an innocent smile.

"I wanted you," she admitted, then added hastily, "to ride with me and point out the highlights." His smile was working its magic on her, making her forget her resolutions to remain emotionally uninvolved.

"Didn't Willie do that?"

"Yes, but it wasn't the same," she answered softly.

"No, it wasn't," he agreed, attracted once again to her openness and warm, likable personality and despising himself for it. It would make his life a whole lot easier if she wasn't so damn perfect.

Their eyes met in silent accord, hinting at what might be, but this was not the time or place to make any promises. A shiver of anticipation shook her slight body. Maybe tonight . . .

"Maybe we could impose on Sunny and get her to sing a few songs for us," someone suggested. Other voices joined in, echoing the encouragement, while several people hurried away to get their guitars.

Sarah felt a surge of panic. She had not anticipated being asked to sing. There must be some way she could get out of this gracefully. Her voice was gentle and sweet, but it had none of the vitality and range of Sunny's. Just one song would expose her as an impostor, and she mustn't let that happen now.

"I'm sorry, but I just couldn't," she stammered.

"What's the matter? Is the star too big to sing for free? Maybe we should all take up a collection and see what her price is," a man suggested sarcastically as he staggered up to her, obviously feeling the effects of several beers too many. A stunned silence settled over the group as he fumbled with his wallet, pulled out a bill, and with a swiftness that could not have been anticipated, stuffed it into the cleavage that was revealed by her tight red jump suit.

The drunk's next move was to pick himself up from the dirt where he lay after Tyler's left fist connected with his jaw. He struggled up, his fists ready, but the deadly glitter in Tyler's eyes penetrated his benumbed senses. Backing away from Tyler's imposing figure, the man stumbled over to the ice chest, picked up another beer, and disappeared outside the fire's circle of light.

"Hey, Ty. He didn't mean anything by it," someone

80

said soothingly. "He's just had a little too much to drink. It's okay if Sunny doesn't want to sing."

Tyler glanced back at Sarah's stricken expression, and as if recognizing her dilemma, he forced himself to relax. "I'm sure Sunny would love to sing for us," he said, causing Sarah to gasp in alarm, "but you folks can't expect her to endanger her voice in this cool, humid night air. She's got a big performance at the rodeo in a few days. Why don't we all sing to her for a change. I'll bet that would be a first."

"I play a mean guitar," Sarah was quick to offer. "It's been a long time since I've been to a sing-along."

Luckily that suggestion met with everyone's approval, and they all seemed to accept Tyler's excuse for her without reproach. Someone thrust a guitar into her hands, which she flipped over and fitted to herself.

Tyler settled back into his chair, studying her quizzically. "There's not too many people that play the guitar with their left hand," he commented. "I noticed you ride left-handed too. I never realized you were a southpaw."

"I've always been left-handed, but I learned to play the guitar with my right hand. It wasn't until I saw Paul McCartney so happily adjusted to being left-handed that I switched back over to what came naturally." Confidently she strummed and tuned the instrument. Sunny had often asked Sarah to accompany her when she sang, but Sarah always refused. She didn't mind sitting in on sessions or playing back-up in the recording studios, but she had never wanted to go on stage with her sister.

More loudly than harmoniously the group sang all the

81

songs they knew and some they didn't. Forgetting the words was no problem, as someone could always come up with substitutes, some of them hilarious. It wasn't until almost midnight, when the fire burned down, the beer ran out, and memories began to dim, that the cheerful group began to dissipate, heading off to bed.

Sarah stretched gracefully as she stood up, Tyler's darkened eyes following her every move. Hastily he cleared his throat and levered himself up off the short stool. "My horse threw a shoe today and split his hoof. That's why I was so late to supper," he explained. "I'd better go check on him again before I turn in for the night."

"I'll go with you if you don't mind," she offered, wanting to strengthen the new bond between them. This should give them a chance to talk privately and maybe reach a new understanding.

Tyler hesitated. He was already feeling like he had been twisted in knots tonight. The gentle fragrance of her perfume had attacked his senses until it threatened his sanity. He, too, wanted to have the opportunity to spend more time with her alone, but he wasn't sure he could trust himself tonight. His guard was down, and it was becoming more difficult every minute he was with her to resist her charms.

He wanted her more than he had ever wanted anything in his life, but his common sense always reminded him that his own self-respect was worth more than a quick one-night stand with a woman who would probably not even remember his name a month from now. Still, he could not deny himself this chance to be with her even for just a few more moments. Surely he could hold his passion in check for that long.

They were almost at her trailer when he answered her at last. "Sure, you can come along. Zena will be glad to see you."

The horses were standing quietly, securely tied to the rope picket line that ran between two trees. Their slumber disturbed, they still managed a friendly nicker as Tyler and Sarah approached.

After saying a proper hello to Zena, Sarah leaned back against her soft snow-white body, watching Tyler attend to his horse's hoof. As he straightened back up he paused, drinking in the sight of her. Bathed in moonlight, the mare seemed to have a ghostly glow, providing a perfect backdrop for the unearthly beauty of the woman reclining against her. There was an innocence about her that the tight suggestive clothes could not hide, but there was also a sensuality just below the surface that had nothing to do with the way she dressed.

Just then his horse shifted, pushing a startled Tyler into an even more surprised Sarah. Automatically his arms wrapped around her, keeping them both from falling. Her soft feminine curves pressed against his taut muscular body. Even after the initial danger was past, neither made a move to break away.

Sarah lifted her face to his, which hovered just inches above hers. "I guess that's what they call animal magnetism," she said as she smiled weakly.

"Thank God for animals," he breathed huskily against her lips.

She met him with a hunger that matched his own and surprised them both. Her long slender fingers locked behind his neck, pulling him even closer. His lips molded to hers as if they had been created to match. Mobilely they moved over hers, drinking in their sweetness like a thirsty man lost in a desert.

This was definitely better than standing next to him washing dishes, she thought. In fact, this was better than anything else she had experienced in her life. Tiny lightning bolts of desire jolted through her body, leaving her weak and shaken but ready for whatever came. His own response was evident as he pressed against her, and she marveled that his physical need was as great as hers. Never again would he be able to convince her that he was unmoved by her presence.

His hand slid down her back, making a strange slippery sound against the satin. His mouth pulled away as he leaned back to study her delicate moonlit face. "Oh, darlin'," he sighed. "What have you done to me?" He pulled her to him again, cradling her against his broad chest, his breath warm against her forehead. "I never expected this or even wanted it to happen. But you've cast some sort of spell over me. I can't seem to resist you." His lips leisurely trailed soft kisses down her neck, and she obligingly turned her head to allow him greater access. "You are so real, so honest," he breathed. "Not at all phony or affected like I would have thought. You've

84

got everyone wrapped around your little finger, me included. You're really someone special."

"But I'm not—" she cried softly.

But he silenced her protests with a kiss. One of his large hands moved up to cup her breast, his thumb rubbing roughly across her nipple, which sent new waves of desire throbbing through her body. Gently his tongue tasted her lips, then ran along the uneven line of her teeth before her mouth surrounded it greedily. His hand wandered to the zipper that held the front of her jump suit closed. His fingers stroked her breasts.

Suddenly he stiffened and pulled away, a crumpled twenty-dollar bill held between his thumb and forefinger as if it were contaminated. "I should have broken his jaw," he growled, and threw it to the ground with obvious disgust.

"You very likely did," she replied shakily. "I meant to thank you for taking up for me like that. And don't say it was just part of your job," she cautioned.

He smiled down at her gently. "I'm getting used to being a knight in blue jeans—as long as I have a beautiful princess to protect. And now, beautiful princess, it's time you got to bed. We're going to have a long day tomorrow, and it's getting very late." He glanced at his watch and amended, "Or rather, very early."

Sarah looked up into his dear face, longing to pour her heart out to him. But this was not the proper time. They both had other things on their minds; probably the same things. She knew it was late, but she didn't want this night to end.

85

Slowly they walked back to her camper, their arms wrapped around each other, their hips rubbing sensuously together with each step.

"Do you want to come in?" she queried lightly as they hesitated outside her door.

"I can't," he whispered, his eyes telling her how much he wanted to, but his brain telling him he had better not.

"I know," she answered regretfully, and she understood his dilemma because she was struggling with one of her own. Once more his lips claimed hers for a tender bittersweet kiss before he left her for the night.

CHAPTER SEVEN

Even though she knew it would be a short night, Sarah was too keyed up to fall asleep quickly. There was a small portable TV in the camper, but the reception was poor, and the selection for late-night viewing was even worse, so she turned it back off. Rummaging through the nightstand cabinet, she uncovered a paperback copy of one of her favorite author's books. She had already seen the movie and had intended to read the book, so she was pleased. She settled into bed with the book, but after only a couple of chapters she lost interest in it too.

Tyler Ross. She savored the name as it forced its way back into her thoughts. One week ago she had never even heard of him, and now she couldn't think of anything else. What was in store for her next week? Since she couldn't see how it could include Tyler, she wasn't anxious to find out.

She tried to remember all the obstacles and complications that would make any personal relationship with Tyler a hopeless dream. Logically she listed them in her mind. Most important, of course, was her obligation to Sunny. Sarah had promised to see this deception through to the end, and she would keep that promise, regardless of the sacrifices.

Tyler, she reminded herself, had made it clear that he was attracted to her—or rather, to Sunny. Even though he seemed to be unimpressed by her star status, Sarah had often seen show business relationships that were based, not on love or mutual respect but on an obsession with being associated with someone rich and famous. And even if Tyler were attracted to Sarah herself, he would be hurt and furious when he discovered that she had deceived him and didn't trust him enough to share the truth with him. But because Sunny's reputation was at stake, Sarah couldn't allow herself the liberty of confessing the truth to him. Besides, it had taken him so long to accept her that if she suddenly revealed that all of his conclusions about her were wrong, she was afraid he would think she had betrayed him like his ex-fiancée and wouldn't give her another chance.

It all boiled down to the old saying that she was damned if she did, and damned if she didn't. She couldn't tell him now, and she was certain that once she did, he would hate her for her dishonesty. Either way, she would never see him again after Saturday.

But she couldn't deny the strong physical attraction he had for her. No man had ever ignited her senses and filled her with a longing so intense that it made her body ache with desire. He didn't even have to touch her to send her pulse racing erratically. He controlled her with his smile or the warm twinkle in his soft gray eyes. There could be no promises for the future, but that didn't lessen her infatuation. She didn't want to go through the rest of her life knowing she had wasted any of the time they had left together.

Tears of frustration welled up in her eyes. If she hadn't agreed to Sunny's outrageous proposition in the first place, she wouldn't have this problem. Of course, if she hadn't pretended to be Sunny, she would never have met Tyler. Would that have been any worse than what she was feeling now? Maybe someday in the future she would be able to think of him, remembering only the joys and forgetting the pain.

She didn't hear reveille that morning, but Tyler's pounding on the trailer door brought her slowly awake. When she finally pulled on her robe and opened the door, he handed her a cup of coffee and a plate filled with hot eggs, sausages, and biscuits, which she put on the table. Then, after glancing furtively behind him to reassure himself that no one was watching them, he leaned into the trailer and kissed her soundly.

His kiss opened her eyes much more effectively than the cup of coffee. She allowed herself the liberty of watching his muscular form as he strode away, whistling cheerfully. She stood just inside the doorway, one hand holding his kiss to her lips while her heart pounded wildly against her other hand, which clutched her robe together modestly.

It was the beginning of a wonderful day. Later in her life when she would think back on all her best days, she would remember this one especially. The weather wasn't so terrific, and she could have used a few more hours sleep, but nothing mattered as long as Tyler stayed by her side.

His horse's hoof had been filed and reshod, and Tyler led him and Zena up to Sarah's trailer just as the other riders were leaving camp. They lagged behind the others, not anxious to share each other with anyone else. The flat, sparsely populated countryside was obscured by a low, thick fog. The light mist swirled around Tyler and Sarah, enveloping them in a phantasmal cocoon. It was all very surrealistic and perfectly suited their shared mood.

The stillness seemed to discourage conversation, and they rode in companionable silence until the sun struggled up to burn away the fog.

"It sure was a short night last night. Did you sleep well?" Tyler asked, curious to know if she had found it as difficult to rest as he had.

"Not really," she admitted with a shy smile. "I tried reading a book, but that didn't help much."

"I believe I did leave a couple of Larry McMurtry books in the bedroom. I read them last summer when I spent a week on Padre Island."

"You've slept in that trailer?" she asked.

"I guess so." He laughed, his even teeth flashing whitely against his tanned skin. "It's my trailer."

"Oh. I never realized that it was yours," she replied, feeling somehow more intimate with him now that she knew she had used his shower and slept in his bed, even though he hadn't been there at the time, of course. "That makes me feel bad, though, knowing that you're sleeping outside while I'm enjoying your camper. It's really much nicer than I would have guessed. I just assumed that the Rodeo Association had provided it for me."

"Don't worry about it," he said. "I always sleep outside with the others on these trail rides. That's part of the fun, I guess. I wouldn't have brought the trailer at all if you hadn't been going to use it."

"If you're sure," she replied, only slightly mollified.

"I'm sure," he stated firmly, then abruptly changed the subject. "You never have leveled with me about where you really learned to handle a horse. You ride much better than I had been led to believe. Or do you fall off horses at rodeos just for the publicity?"

"Everyone has bad days," she said, defending Sunny. "Actually I grew up around horses. My father is a horse trainer who still works for one of the most successful Thoroughbred racing stables in Kentucky. He really loves it and is very good. They've won hundreds of major races and even the Triple Crown once. I used to dream of being a jockey until I grew up a little too much."

"So your father let you ride the horses he was training?"

"He didn't just let me ride. I worked with him. I would get up before dawn and exercise four or five horses before school every day and spend all day Saturday at the racetracks during the season."

"An odd sort of life for a girl who would one day be a country and western singer," he commented wryly.

"That life was certainly no worse than living in hotels and spending half my time in smoky clubs and concert halls. Back then I lived, breathed, and slept horses. But then 'Daddy's Baby' hit it big, followed by my first Grammy Award and three more Top 40 singles in a row. Since then I've been on the road more than I've been home, and that doesn't give me a chance to ride much. Certainly not as much as I would like."

"Have you enjoyed your life as a celebrity?"

"Oh, sure. It has its advantages. I think everyone has fantasized about being in the limelight in one way or another. For some people fame is their destiny. It's as if they couldn't escape it even if they wanted to, which in most cases they don't. They know they must take the bad with the good, but it's worth it to them."

"Is it worth it to you? Would you live your life any differently if you had the chance?" He watched her face intensely, fascinated by the medley of emotions written there.

"My case is not typical. My sister and I were brought up in a loving, religious atmosphere, and it has given us a strong, solid background. We haven't had to deal with the panic of being all alone against the world because we've got each other and our parents ready to catch us if we fall. This built-in security system has helped us avoid many of the pitfalls associated with show business."

"You'd never know that by what is reported by the press," Tyler commented. "From what I've heard about Sunny Day, she's given a new meaning to the expression 'one-night stand.' "

"Publicity is what makes showbiz go round. With it we're infamous, without it we're nobodies." Sarah shrugged. "It's a no-win situation. If we ignore bad press, people assume it's true, but if we deny it, they think we doth protest too much."

" 'Contradiction is not a sign of falsity, nor the lack of contradiction a sign of truth,' " he quoted sagely.

"That's very true," she agreed. "Do you want to hear my favorite quotation?"

"Sure," he answered, viewing the mischievous twinkle in her eyes somewhat suspiciously.

"Never play leapfrog with a unicorn," she stated solemnly.

"I've always lived by the proverb that if you eat a live toad the first thing in the morning, nothing worse will happen to you the rest of the day," he responded, then burst into laughter at her horrified expression.

"How about never eat at a place called Mom's, never play cards with a man named Ace, and never invest in anything that eats or needs painting," she challenged.

"That's not fair. You sneaked in three that time," he protested. "Have you heard that when you're in it up to your nose, you should keep your mouth shut?"

"You can lead a horse to water, but if you can get him to float on his back, you've really achieved something." She giggled.

An exchange of frivolous quotations followed, sending them both into gales of hysterical laughter. They were obviously having such a good time that others were attracted, and soon Tyler and Sarah were surrounded by a small group shouting questions and answers back and forth. The subject shifted to movies, television shows, and famous theme songs.

Even when they were no longer alone, Sarah and Tyler hung on to their invisible bond. When their eyes met, he would slip her a very personal wink and she would reward him with a secret smile. The time passed much too quickly.

After they finished lunch, Tyler commented, "You had better bring along your coat this afternoon. You may have the chance to experience one of our famous blue northerns before nightfall."

Sarah looked doubtfully at the clear blue skies overhead. As she glanced toward the north, however, she saw a dark bluish gray cloud bank splashed low along the horizon, as if an artist had brushed the paint on too dark and forgotten to blend it in. "It looks like it's still a long way from us. When do you think it will hit?"

"I heard on the weather report that this was an arctic cold front that was moving pretty fast. We should be feeling the winds and the rain within a few hours. By sundown the temperature should drop into the forties with a freeze predicted for tonight," he explained while unhobbling the horses.

"When it decides to get cold, it doesn't waste any time, does it?"

"It's been said that Houston has only two seasons: summer and February." He chuckled. "I can't remember a Salt Grass Trail Ride that hasn't been rained on or frozen. We've been lucky for the past few days."

"Yes, we have," she whispered, too low for him to hear, but she wasn't referring to the weather.

The front blew in even quicker and meaner than expected. They were still about a mile from their campsite in Katy Park when the winds switched from a mild southwest breeze to a roaring northern blast.

Sarah had commented earlier on the wide range in the ages of the trail riders, and Tyler had told her that the youngest this year was not yet two years old and the oldest was Willie at seventy-eight. All ages in between were represented, both male and female. But this change in the weather seemed to separate the men from the boys, in a manner of speaking.

Mothers bundled their children into the backs of the covered wagons, and soon the fainthearted of all ages joined them. A much depleted group, consisting of only the truly dedicated and the very foolish, was left on the trail.

Sarah wasn't certain which group she fell into, but she was determined to make it all the way to Katy Park. Tyler tried to talk her into joining the crowds in the backs of the wagons, but she refused to listen. If he could make it, so could she. She pulled the heavy yellow slicker on over her coat and persistently stayed at his side as they stepped up the pace in an attempt to make it to camp before the rain hit.

Although everyone was prepared for the rain, wearing the yellow slickers that had been tied behind their saddles, they were surprised at the velocity and fury of the storm as it enveloped them wetly. The riders were forced to slow down as they neared the camp, following the leader blindly, their coats the only bright spots in the dismal gray landscape.

The wind drove the cold pelting rain against their left sides and backs. Even with their shoulders hunched forward and their hats pulled down low, the rain managed to run down their necks. Nothing could stop the cold that seemed to penetrate their bones.

Sarah was beginning to doubt the sanity of her decision when, at last, the welcome sight of the assembled vehicles came into view. A large tarpaulin had been erected to form meager protection from the elements for Jed's chuck wagon. Eagerly the riders crowded under the shelter, helping themselves to the steaming hot coffee that was waiting for them.

Sarah literally slid off Zena's slick saddle and into Tyler's waiting arms. Even though she was cold and wet, the reassuring touch of his large hands around her waist was enough to send a warming flash through her body. His hand moved up to stroke her numbed cheek before lifting her chin so that she met his admiring gray gaze.

"You look like a drowned rat, your makeup is running, and I've never seen anything more beautiful in my life," he whispered huskily.

Sarah choked on a giggle. "Thanks, I think. Possibly there was a compliment hidden in there somewhere, but I've never heard a more left-handed one."

"A left-handed compliment for a left-handed lady," he quipped. "Let's see how you interpret this." His breath brushed her wet lips a split second before his mouth told her what his words had not conveyed. Oblivious to the rain that trickled down their faces, they shared the desire that flowed hotly through their blood as their kiss deepened dangerously. Showing remarkable restraint, Tyler took a step backward. "Unless you want to make the front page of the *Houston Post* tomorrow, you'd better let me go take care of the horses. I want you to go straight to your camper and get dried off. I'll let you know when supper is ready."

"I'm going to get a cup of coffee first. I'll see you later, unless you feel the urge to give me another compliment right now." She flashed him a seductive smile.

"You'd better get away from here right now, or I guarantee you the front page of not only both Houston papers but the *National Enquirer* too," he threatened with a wolfish grin.

"Promises, promises . . ." she tossed saucily over her shoulder as she wisely left him with the horses.

Jed had set up his cooking area so that the worst of the wind and rain was blocked off on two sides by vehicles and natural cover. The heat from the cooking fires radiated surprising warmth and provided immediate relief from the storm.

After pouring herself a cup of coffee Sarah dreaded the thought of going back out in the weather even for so short a trip as to her trailer. When Jed announced that supper was ready, she decided she might as well fix herself a plate and take it with her.

There was thick Texas chili that Jed guaranteed would "warm your innards and stick to your ribs" and pans of hot crumbly cornbread. Jed's cooking was meant to be eaten only by Tyler and his group, as everyone else on the trail ride was expected to prepare their own meals. But tonight, lured by the tantalizing smell and the protective cover, several extras joined in to help empty the huge cast-iron pot. Sarah noticed that Jed had set aside generous portions for Tyler and the others who were still out with the horses.

The weather continued to worsen as the temperature dipped toward freezing. With the winds sustaining their fury at over twenty miles per hour, the wind chill factor made it seem closer to zero. The shivering riders huddled around a portable TV, listening to the weather forecaster warning of severe weather conditions through Thursday with the temperature continuing to drop and a high of only thirty predicted. To make matters even worse, rain mixed with sleet would continue until midmorning.

Curses were muttered through stiff lips as the riders dispersed to try to make themselves and their animals as comfortable as possible for the savage night ahead. Willie had been standing next to Sarah but now turned to follow the rest.

"Will Ethyl be okay tonight?" Sarah asked, concerned for the ancient mule and even more worried about her old master.

"Me and Ethyl's been through worse weather than this. Besides, Ethyl's spending the night in Ty's horse trailer with a blanket and everything. That mule will probably be so spoiled, she won't even talk to me tomorrow," he said with a snort.

"And what about you, Willie? Where will you be sleeping?" she questioned gently.

"Oh, I've got me a good sleeping bag, and I'm goin' to crawl up into one of them wagons. By the time I fall asleep, I'll have enough antifreeze in me to last till March, anyway," he said with a cackle, silencing her protests with a wave of his hand. "It's right nice of you to worry about old Willie. Not too many folks pay me much attention, you know. But, hey, I'll be fine."

Sarah watched him disappear into the darkness, hoping he knew what he was doing. Tyler had still not returned from bedding down the horses, but she decided she shouldn't wait for him here any longer. She had hoped to see him again tonight, but he had warned her he would be very busy preparing for the continuing storm. She called a good-night to Jed and the cowboys who still huddled around the fire finishing their meal, and went into her trailer.

Some wonderful person had turned the heat up high, and she was welcomed into a blissful warmth. Eagerly she peeled off her clinging clothes, tossed them into a pile, followed them up with her hat and scraggly wig, and stepped into a steaming shower. It took several minutes for feeling to come back into her numbed body. It wasn't until the small hot water tank was completely empty that Sarah left the shower. She dried off leisurely, toweling the moisture from her long hair.

This was one of the first times this week she had truly appreciated her sister's star status and preferential treatment. She tried not to think about those less fortunate who would be sleeping in unheated tents or wagons, especially Tyler. It wasn't exactly fair that she should be enjoying his camper while he roughed it in the cold. She would gladly share the warmth with him, but he hadn't asked, and she didn't know if she was willing to make that all-important first move.

Feelings of frustration made her unreasonably restless. She found some hot chocolate mix and made herself a cup that she ended up leaving almost untouched as she struggled to repair the damage to Sunny's wig. At last, when even her experienced hands couldn't make it look as good as it should, Sarah decided to wash it tonight and restyle it tomorrow. After washing it and toweling it dry she hung it in the bathroom and tried again to read the book she had started the night before.

The noisy clatter of frozen rain against her windows and on the metal roof of the trailer was a constant reminder of the unfriendly weather conditions, and she hoped again that wherever Tyler was, he was comfortable and dry. Just as she had decided to turn off the light and try to get some sleep, even though the prospect seemed highly unlikely, a new sound brought her scrambling to the window.

The wind had ripped the tarpaulin from its moorings, leaving one corner to snap back and forth, sounding very much like a whip cracking. As she watched, Tyler, Jed, and several others ran out and, sensing a futile fight against the wind and sleet, unfastened the other three corners, folded it up, and took down the poles.

Watching them struggle against the uncooperative elements made Sarah shiver sympathetically. She moved away, letting the curtain drop back into place, but she could still hear their shouts, which were thrown toward her by the wind, even though she couldn't understand what they were saying. A few minutes later she heard several vehicles start up and drive away from camp.

Sarah was just getting up to look out the window again when she heard a knock at the trailer door. Pulling on her robe, she went to the door but hesitated, a little frightened that she should have a visitor so late.

"It's me, Tyler," he called in answer to her unspoken question. "Are you still awake?"

Her hands fumbled with the lock before she opened the door and stared at him in dismay. Still wearing his yellow slicker and soaked jeans, he looked miserable and uncharacteristically vulnerable. His face had a strange pale, almost blue pallor and tiny icicles hung from the brim of his sodden hat.

"I saw your light was still on and wondered if there was something wrong. Do you need anything?" he asked, his teeth clenched from the cold.

Her heart cried out to him, *I need you,* but aloud she said, "I'm fine, but what about you? Where are you going to sleep tonight?"

"I sent my men to a motel, except for Jed. He wanted to stay here with his chuck wagon, and someone has to take care of you, so he's going to sleep in his chuck wagon, and I'm going to sleep in the cab of the pickup truck." His breath billowed in a white cloud as he spoke.

"Oh, no, you're not," Sarah exclaimed, opening the door wide. "You're going to sleep in here tonight."

"Oh, no, I'm not." He shook his head, sending sprinkles of ice off his hat. "I don't think that would be a very good idea for either of us."

"You're freezing out there, and it's nice and warm in here. There's absolutely no reason why you shouldn't stay here," she argued.

"I can think of several right offhand," he retorted. "There's your reputation, for one thing."

"That's baloney," she countered. "I think you're more worried about *your* reputation. Besides Jed, who would know anyway? I promise I won't ever mention it to anyone, not even the supermarket rags," she teased.

"You know it isn't that." His eyes eloquently raked her scantily clad figure. "I'm sure that in spite of the discomfort and the cold I could get more sleep cramped in the pickup truck than here in the room next to you."

"We're both adults." She forced her voice to remain calm. "There's one bed in the bedroom, and I'm sure that this is a sleeper sofa, so we can work something out."

"That's exactly what I'm afraid of," he responded more harshly than he intended.

"Would you please come in before I freeze to death! The longer we argue, the greater the risk that I'll catch pneumonia, which I would blame entirely on you." She had decided to appeal to his sense of duty. "I won't take no for an answer," she added firmly.

For a moment longer he hesitated, his eyes reflecting his inward conflict. She didn't realize what physical pain she had already put him through, or that now she was insisting that he add to the torture. She was just making a kind, generous gesture with no hidden meanings intended. No matter how badly he wanted her, he was a mature man, and surely he was capable of controlling his passion for one night.

"Like I said before, lady, you're the boss." He shrugged with renewed resolve as he knocked the clumps of mud off his boots and stepped into the trailer.

CHAPTER EIGHT

Sarah pulled off Tyler's soggy boots and helped him get out of his stiff slicker and heavy suede leather coat, which she hung near the door so they could drip on the vinyl floor of the small entryway instead of on the carpet. Both of them were taking extra pains not to touch each other, sensing the possible explosiveness of the situation. Tension filled the room like an overblown balloon waiting for the tiniest pinprick of passion to burst it.

Tyler turned on the range burners and, after discarding his gloves, held his frozen hands over the warming flames, turning his back on Sarah in an attempt to force his hungry eyes from her unconsciously seductive figure. Resisting her tonight was going to take the self-control of a saint, and he certainly was no saint!

Absolutely not, he lectured himself. *You will not make a fool of yourself by letting desire get the better of your self-respect.* He refused to become just another notch on her guitar. His teeth gritted together in determination as he forced himself to repeat that statement over and over until he thought he had himself convinced. But when he turned around to confront his nemesis, his firm jaw dropped open in despair.

Sarah had taken some sheets from the cabinet over the sofa, which she had pulled out to make into a bed, and was leaning over it, engrossed in tucking the sheets under the cushions. Tyler's view, however, was limited to her well-rounded derriere, emphasized by the off-white silk clinging to her enticing curves.

"Damn!" he growled, his breath escaping in a rush from his suddenly malfunctioning lungs. His first impulse was to leap across the small room, throw her on the half-made couch, and make wild, passionate love to her. His second impulse was to flee before his first impulse became fact.

"What?" Sarah straightened, looking at him with wide eyes. "Are you okay?" she asked, alarmed by the strange, strangled look on his face. She took a step toward him, her hand outstretched.

"I need to take a shower," he stated, almost frantically avoiding her touch. "Do you mind?"

"Of course not. After all, it is your shower." She continued to watch him curiously. "I used all the hot water earlier, but it should be replaced by now."

"The colder the better," he muttered, and hastily fled from the room.

Sarah shook her head, bewildered by his bizarre behavior. She heard the pump kick on and muffled sounds coming from the shower. With a shrug she finished making the bed and put a pot of water on to boil so coffee would be ready for Tyler when he returned.

He seemed to be in a much more normal frame of mind when he rejoined her after a long shower. But now it was Sarah's turn to feel discomfort as she stared at his half-naked body. Unaware of her devouring stare, he was briskly rubbing his hair dry with a towel. She welcomed the opportunity to gaze unchecked at his magnificent male form. Her appreciative eyes feasted on the breadth of his shoulders, his bulging biceps, the thick dark hair covering the convex curve of his chest, trickling down the middle of his stomach, and disappearing behind the thick blue towel that swathed his narrow hips. Long sinewy legs a couple of shades paler than his tanned torso were visible beneath the almost too short towel.

"All my clothes were wet," he commented with a crooked apologetic grin as he saw her aghast expression. "I hung them up in the bathroom to dry."

She didn't trust herself to speak, so instead she busied herself mixing the hot water with the instant coffee in the mugs. She breathed a sigh of relief when he sat down at the table, temporarily putting most of himself out of her view. Now she had only his ruggedly handsome face with its direct gray gaze and gently curving mouth to contend with in her crazy runaway thoughts.

He had raked his fingers roughly through his thick ebony hair, combing it back from his face, but a stray lock hung wetly across his forehead, begging to be brushed back into place by her itching fingers. Abruptly she sat down on her chair, before her weak knees could collapse beneath her.

"It was a little unnerving to be taking a shower and to

turn around and see a horrible hairy blond thing hanging from the towel bar," he said, attempting to lighten the atmosphere.

"I'm not sure it can be saved." She laughed nervously. "The most humane thing would probably be to shoot it and put it out of its misery."

"I don't believe I've ever seen any pictures of you au naturel."

"I beg your pardon?" she asked, shocked. "I would never agree to do nude photos." She glared indignantly at him.

"No, wait," he said soothingly. "I meant without that wig. You really do have beautiful hair." His approving gaze swept the long, loose length of spun gold that tumbled down around her breasts. "I wonder how many people know what you've been hiding all these years," he speculated, his tone suggesting a more complex curiosity than his words would indicate.

Indirectly he was asking her how many people she had been intimate enough with to share this secret. If only she could get up enough courage to tell him what other secrets were hidden beneath that artificial hairpiece. Not that it was really any of his business, but she couldn't blame him for asking. If she'd had the nerve to ask, she would have loved to find out the same information about him. Instead "Sunny Day" stayed in character. "Not as many as you might think. Other than my family and my manager, Mack, no one ever sees me without my wig."

"That makes me special, then, doesn't it?" he teased

lightly, but the joke backfired as her eyes darkened seriously.

"Yes, it does," she answered softly. Several seconds passed, their gazes locked, with neither daring to say what was foremost in their minds. Sarah moved first, scooting her chair away from the table noisily and walking over to the sink to rinse out her mug. "It's getting late. I guess we had better turn in for the night, so if you'll just go on into the bedroom—"

"The bedroom?" he interrupted, one dark eyebrow arched eloquently.

"Yes, you'll sleep in the bedroom, and I'll sleep on the sofa," she finished hastily.

"Oh." He tried to hide his disappointment in the sleeping arrangements. "I believe you've got it backward, though," he argued.

"No, I don't. It's your camper, and you're too tall for the sofa, so it's just common sense for me to sleep on the sofa and let you have the bed."

"You bullied me into spending the night in this camper, but I refuse to let you give up the bed. I know that you're not on a star trip, but you, as a woman, will sleep on the bed, and I, as a man, will rough it on the sofa." His deep voice demanded obedience. "Either that or I'll sleep in the truck. Then you can sleep in whichever bed you want."

"Male chauvinist!" she accused.

"Superstar!" he countered.

"All right, take the sofa," she acquiesced, knowing that if she didn't, he would make good his threat to go back outside into the bitter cold, sleep in the truck, and probably catch the flu—a fate he deserved, but one which she couldn't wish on him. With a defiant toss of her golden head she flounced gracefully from the room.

An hour later she lay on her back on the big bed, staring into the dark. Her only excuse for her childish behavior was that it had effectively disguised her real feelings. She had narrowly escaped from a very tense sexual confrontation. So why was she still awake, feeling every emotion but satisfaction? Hadn't she been acting in Sunny's best interests? Or was she just afraid to admit that her whole body ached for a fulfillment that only this man could provide? She had never been stirred so deeply and passionately, which made her doubly vulnerable. If she overreacted to what she thought was a sexual overture but wasn't, then he would think she was as loose and forward as her sister had a reputation for being. She tried to remember anything he might have said or done that could give her a clue as to how he felt, but other than their few kisses his behavior had always been that of a perfect gentleman . . . unfortunately.

From the other room came the sound of Tyler turning over and bumping loudly into the wooden arms at either the head or foot of his too short bed and uttering a most ungentlemanly curse. It served him right, she thought. Apparently he wasn't getting any more sleep than she was, but it was all his fault. If he had listened to reason, he'd be able to stretch his long frame out on this bed, and she would have been quite comfortable on the smaller sofa.

Maybe now he would be a little more open-minded, she told herself as she got out of bed and flicked on the overhead light. Maybe she could talk him into playing musical beds. That was her only reason for going to see him now, in the middle of the night, wasn't it? Sarah opened the bedroom door but paused on the threshold.

Tyler saw her immediately and sat up, leaning on one elbow. Shafts of light broke around her body, piercing through the thin gown, making it virtually invisible. Her hair fell around her shoulders and down almost to her elbows in glorious disarray, highlighted from behind like a frothy halo. Her face was in shadow, making it impossible to read her expression, but he sensed a tense indecision. She was like a shy doe, poised for flight at the first sign of danger. He wasn't sure why she was here, but a wave of passion surged through his body with the power and fierceness of the wild north wind that had shown them no mercy earlier in the day, just as she was showing him no mercy now.

"I couldn't sleep. I wondered if you . . ." She faltered, all coherent thoughts driven from her mind at the sight of him. The light from her bedroom invaded the dark room, softly illuminating his tanned nude torso in sharp contrast to the whiteness of the sheets.

All his well-planned resolutions flew out the window. His eyes, burning with desire, never left her face as he reached out and pulled back the covers to expose the empty space next to him. "Come here, darlin'," he invited, his voice deep and gentle as he held out his hand toward her.

Still Sarah hesitated, weighing the possible results against the depth of her desire. What would happen if he should expect the real Sunny to pick up where they left off after the trail ride was over? Or what if he let something slip to the press that might hurt Sunny's career? Or what if . . . Suddenly she realized that for this one night she didn't really care about anything else but Tyler. Regardless of the repercussions this was her one chance to be where she most wanted to be: in his arms. Tonight was their night; she would worry about everything else tomorrow.

With a soft heartfelt sigh she floated across the room and sank into his waiting arms.

His body shuddered with suppressed longing as he looked deeply into her apprehensive eyes. "Are you sure?" he asked tenderly.

"Shh," she whispered against his lips, her body melting against his warmth. She had gone this far, and she didn't want to be talked out of it now. This was not the moment for rational thoughts. For once sensible Sarah was going to let her heart rule her head.

Tentatively, not wanting to overwhelm her with the strength of his feelings, Tyler gently kissed her mouth while his hands slowly stroked her body.

But Sarah wanted more. She had been waiting for this moment since she had first been attracted to him at the airport. Boldly her fingertips slid down the hard curve of his side and up the ridge of his hipbone. She savored the rippling waves of muscles in his back and shoulders before her long fingers nested in the thick silken hair at the back of his neck. Her lips pulled him deeper into the kiss, demanding everything he had to give.

"Take it easy. We've got all night," he murmured against her mouth as his hands eased under the hem of her gown, drawing it up and with her help pulling it over her head before tossing it on the floor. He pulled away and leaned back so he could see the uncharted territory waiting to be explored and conquered. His passion-darkened eyes flowed over her body, lingering on her firm, full breasts, which swelled expectantly under his warm gaze.

"Thank God that only your wig is artificial," he teased, his large, rough palm following the same path as his eyes. His forefinger traced lazy circles around the pink tips of her nipples before he leaned over to sample their nectar. His tongue teased and tantalized the hardened buds as he divided his avid attention between them.

Sarah uttered a soft cry of delight. Her fingers tightened on his powerful shoulders, urging him to continue. Her long silky legs entwined with his, enjoying the sensual tickle of the light sprinkling of hair on his legs.

A growing ache throbbed deep within her, sending jolting flashes of pleasure shooting through her as his hot, eager mouth sucked and nibbled until she thought she would go wild with desire. His exploring hand moved down across her flat stomach, then slipped lower, finding her warmth.

His lips ended their torture and moved up to recapture her open mouth, swallowing her entranced moans. Their warm panting breaths mixed as his tongue erotically

112

stroked the roof of her mouth. Her body trembled as the driving ache inside her begged for fulfillment.

Sensing her readiness and unable to hold himself back any longer, Tyler eased his body over hers, gently positioning himself between her legs. His mouth continued its seduction of her soul as their hearts thudded wildly in unison.

The muscles of her throat and chest constricted, making it difficult to breathe as a delicious sense of anticipation pounded through her body. Her gasp of pleasure was mixed with pain as he entered her.

"Relax," he crooned, thinking her withdrawal was due to hesitancy. He slowed his movements, trying to be gentle and patient in spite of the rising urgency that was threatening to overwhelm him. But as he pushed deeper he felt a telltale resistance that caused him to pull back, surprised and confused. "How could you be . . . ?"

She stopped his untimely inquisition by pressing her shaking fingertips against his open lips. "Please don't stop," she pleaded softly, her index finger lightly outlining the sensual curve of his captivating mouth. "I need you . . . now."

Instinctively her legs crossed behind him, holding him to her as her hands moved down his arched back, stopping to stroke and knead the tensed muscles of his buttocks, not so subtly urging him to resume his delightful possession of her body.

With a groan he continued his gentle assault, until with one thrust he accepted her gift, possessing her as no man ever had. Greedily his kiss ravaged her mouth until his lips moved in an open caress across her cheek and against her ear, where his labored breathing rasped seductively.

Her fingers stroked the pulsating tendons in his powerful thighs, encouraging him to a greater intimacy. The sensitive tips of her breasts pressed into the soft, dark hair on his chest as her body rose anxiously against his. All her senses were heightened to such a fever pitch that even her toes curled as his thrust deepened and his pace quickened. He ignited a wildfire of unimaginable sensations swirling in ever widening circles from deep in the pit of her stomach until she was consumed by the flames. Time ceased to exist as agonizingly exciting explosions rippled through her, pulling Tyler with her through the black void.

Weakly he clung to her while deep shudders shook his body. Slowly they returned to earth, lying quietly in each other's arms, tired but satisfied. As their erratic breathing calmed they became aware of the wind that continued to howl as it nudged the trailer and rattled the windows, making the lovers doubly grateful to be sharing each other's warmth.

Tyler nuzzled her neck while one of his hands gently stroked her silky tangled hair. "You are one of the most confusing, exasperating, and completely irresistible women I have ever met," he murmured huskily. "I didn't want to have anything to do with you. I thought you would be full of tricks and shenanigans that would cause this week to be pure torture, but I never suspected the torture would be physical or that you would be so—" He

114

searched for the proper word, then settled on "real. I tried not to think about you except in an official capacity, but I've had very unprofessional thoughts about you since that first night in the motel room when all I saw was long golden hair and even longer sexy legs. Not even in my wildest dreams did I think it could be this special."

She sighed in agreement, the power of speech somehow escaping her while she lay in contented languor, his large body still half-covering hers. Stubbornly she refused to let the nagging voice of her conscience intrude on this perfect moment. Sooner or later Tyler would demand an explanation of her inexperience, and she would need all her wits about her to keep up the facade. But for now this night in his arms was all she wanted. She hoped he would have the sensitivity not to pursue the matter of her innocence at this moment, thus shattering the fragile bond they had just forged.

Although that was the subject that was foremost in his mind, Tyler wisely decided the time was not right for questions. Her innocence intrigued and excited him. His hunger for her was proving to be insatiable as he gloried in the softness of her hair against his cheek and her fresh, intoxicating fragrance, which filled his nostrils. His heartbeat had barely returned to its normal cadence and already he was feeling a renewed stirring of desire for her as she snuggled against him, one of her hands idly combing the dark curls on his chest. He moved, trying to straighten his cramped legs, but only succeeded in bumping his head against the armrest. "Ow," he complained, a pained look crossing his face in a boyishly appealing expression as he rubbed the point of contact with his hand.

"Poor baby," she cooed unsympathetically. "Well, so much for the sofa. Will you agree to move to the bed now?"

"Only if you'll share it with me," he bargained.

"I wouldn't want it any other way." Her long lashes lowered seductively as she spoke.

"The lengths some women will go to to prove their point," he pretended to grumble as he gathered her temptingly nude body up into his strong arms.

"Sometimes a woman has to make a few sacrifices to prove that she is right," she teased, locking her arms around his neck and pressing her full breasts against his chest.

" 'Tis better to suffer and win than never to play at all," Tyler said gravely.

"Was that Emerson?" she guessed, a tiny frown creasing her forehead as she tried to identify the quote.

"No, that was Tyler Ross." He laughed. "Let's go do a little more suffering on the bed." His demanding lips pressed hotly against her neck. "From now on that sofa will be saved for company."

"Oh, no!" Sarah stiffened, almost twisting out of his grasp as she turned her head to peer into his face. "Poor Willie has probably frozen to death in the back of one of those drafty old wagons. Maybe you should go get him and insist that he spend the rest of the night on the sofa."

Tyler was touched by the genuine concern in her voice. This woman was a strange mixture of contradictions that

116

defied all his preconceived notions about her. "Don't worry about old Willie. He was feeling no pain when my men picked him up and took him to the motel with them. Sometimes he can be as stubborn and ornery as that mule of his, so we had to wait until his resistance was too low for him to refuse us."

"That is obviously a tactic at which you are very proficient," she commented, nibbling the sharp line of his collarbone.

Gently he lowered her to the bed, his own body following hers onto the roomy queen-size mattress. "So tell me, darlin'," he asked, his voice a low, husky rumble against her breasts, "how low is *your* resistance right now?"

"Too low to refuse you anything," she murmured against his lips as her body fit perfectly against his, answering his throbbing desire.

The unwelcome blare of reveille roused them from their slumber. It hadn't been very long since they had fallen into an exhausted sleep, still wrapped in each other's arms. Sarah stretched lazily, unaware of the sensual appeal of her sleek creamy body and golden mane of hair. With a low moan of renewed hunger for a taste of her luscious assets, Tyler tightened his hold on her and began to devour her sleepy swollen lips.

Their lovemaking was leisurely but thorough, sending them soaring together through the mist of mutual fulfillment. Sarah had never realized how empty and one-dimensional her life had been before she met Tyler. She loved his warmth, his humor, and his tenderness, not to

117

mention that he looked pretty darn good in or out of a towel.

If she could be sure that he wouldn't reject her as he had his fiancée, she would tell him everything. But it had taken her so long to get him to trust her that she had no doubt that her admission would bring all his anger and disgust flooding back with such force that it would kill whatever budding feelings he might have for her. It was clear that he placed a great deal of value on honesty. It was equally clear to her that there was only one course which, although painful, would provide her with the first totally selfish happiness she had had since childhood. If she wanted Tyler at all, then she must accept the situation as it was and make the most of it because the memories might have to last her a lifetime.

"A dollar for your thoughts," Tyler said softly while his fingertips continued to lightly trace the angles and curves of her lovely face.

Sarah forced aside her melancholy thoughts as she spoke: "A dollar? Whatever happened to a penny?" Her large aquamarine eyes sparkled as she gazed at him affectionately.

"Inflation." He chuckled. "Now tell me what made you look so sad and withdrawn."

"Oh, I was just thinking how strange it will be to rejoin the real world next week. It's too bad we couldn't stay here forever, pretending that nothing outside these walls existed," she mused. "If it hadn't been for that sadist with his recording of reveille this morning, we could have made believe that we were the only survivors in a frozen world."

"And our duty was to repopulate the earth." He perked up, intrigued at the prospect. "But that would mean that all our friends would be frozen like human Popsicles."

"And momsicles." She giggled.

"And horsesicles," he added, then affectionately crushed her against his broad chest while gales of silly laughter shook their bodies. As they quieted they became aware of silence outside the trailer. Apparently last night's storm had passed, taking with it the unwelcome rain and chilling winds and forcing an unwanted break in their temporary isolation.

"Unfortunately"—Tyler struggled to be sensible—"the other riders are going to be returning soon, and I'm not good at making up explanations about why I went into your camper last night and didn't come out again until breakfast. Lying never has been one of my strong suits. I believe it's always better not to get myself into a situation that would force me to be dishonest. Besides, I really should go check on Jed and the horses."

Sarah stretched again, her back arched and her breasts pointing provocatively toward the ceiling. "If you must go, I guess there's no way I can stop you," she teased with a flutter of her long, thick lashes.

"Oh, God," he said with a groan. "Don't do that to me." Playfully he gently bit one of her taut pink nipples. "If there weren't so many eyes focused on your every move, I wouldn't care if we didn't leave this camper until

119

spring. But since I'm the responsible person that I am, I'm going to take a rain check on ravaging your irresistible body until a more inconspicuous time."

"That was a very impressive speech," she said tauntingly, a smile curving her full lips. "I think I'll just spend the whole day in bed, keeping it nice and warm and praying for rain."

Giving her a loud but painless slap on her well-rounded behind, he ordered, "Get your buns out of bed," a wide white smile softening his blow. "I'm going to take another shower. You could join me, and with a little imagination we could pretend it was rain."

"Ha!" She pushed him out of bed. "That shower is too small for one person, let alone a revival of 'Singing in the Rain.' "

"I'll make sure my next camper has a huge bathroom," he grumbled good-naturedly as he rolled athletically to his feet. "But you can't stay here all day. Just thinking about you lying on this bed, so beautiful and desirable . . . Well, I wouldn't be able to stop drooling long enough to carry on a decent conversation."

"I certainly wouldn't want to have that on my conscience." She laughed merrily. "Okay, I'll get up, but you had better leave me some hot water so I can take a shower before I get dressed."

"Only if I can watch."

"You're insatiable, cowboy!" she taunted with pretended exasperation.

"Last night I was a male chauvinist and now I'm insatiable. It's difficult to say whether or not that's an improvement." His dark head was cocked to one side as he pretended to ponder the question.

"I wasn't complaining." She tossed her golden tresses saucily and slapped him soundly on his bare bottom as he stepped toward the bathroom.

Later, when he walked out of the bedroom, the mouth-watering smell of cooking food made his hungry stomach growl enthusiastically. But her slim body barely disguised beneath the clinging gossamer robe hardly completed a typical domestic scene. Even the towel tied around her small waist as a makeshift apron did little to hide her charms. Her hair swirled loosely around her shoulders, rippling as she moved like a waterfall turned golden under the midas touch of the morning sun that sneaked between the cracks of the pulled curtains at the kitchen window.

His indrawn breath whistled through his clenched teeth as the thought slipped through his mind of how nice it would be if it were possible for every morning to be just like this one. But he knew better than to pretend that he could compete with the excitement and personal gratification that the constant travel and adoration gave Sunny. She had said on *Good Morning Houston* that entertaining was vital to her existence. Not only would it not be fair of him to ask her to consider giving it up for him, but he would never feel sure that she wasn't having second thoughts and resenting his interference in her life. Tyler knew from experience that if a woman was truly set on having a successful career, she would let nothing and no one get in her way. There was no way he was going to let another career woman tear his life apart again.

Nonetheless, as hard as he had struggled against becoming involved with this woman, it had happened. Yet how could he possibly regret even one moment he had spent with this surprisingly passionate and interesting female? He knew it was more than just sexual satisfaction that made him want to lock the door against any intrusions from the outside world. But it would be wrong to cage a beautiful songbird, not allowing it to fly or sing as it was born to do.

Today was Thursday, and the parade was Saturday morning. That left only two more days and two more nights to enjoy her company. He was a man of pride and passion, not usually so willing to accept whatever favors a woman chose to bestow upon him, but this woman was special—one of a kind.

"What are you staring at?" Sarah asked over her shoulder. "Haven't you ever seen anyone cooking breakfast before? Don't just stand in the doorway. Come on in and sit down so you can eat while everything's still hot."

"It's just that there is not the remotest resemblance between you and Jed, even though I've watched him cook a hundred meals," Tyler said, recovering his poise and sitting down at the table.

"I'm going to have to thank Jed for stocking the refrigerator so well. It may not be gourmet, but it should hold you until lunch." With a flourish she set a plate of biscuits and a still sizzling pan of sausage on the table next to the butter and orange juice.

"It looks good," he commented, a little doubtful as he helped himself.

"Don't look so skeptical." She grinned. "Anyone can fry sausage and bake whopum biscuits."

"Whopum biscuits?"

"Sure. You just take the can out of the refrigerator, peel the paper off, and whop um against the edge of the counter."

"You suckered me into another one." His deep chuckle pleased her. "I guess this is fresh-squeezed orange juice too."

"It is if it counts that I squeezed the can while I was pouring it into the pitcher."

His laughing gray eyes met hers appreciatively. "Well, Sunny Day, is there no end to your talents?"

For some illogical reason hearing him call her by Sunny's name hurt like a physical blow. She longed to shout, "My name is Sarah, not Sunny, and I love you as I've never loved anyone before," but duty made her swallow those words.

Instead she murmured, "I'm sure you don't have enough time right now for me to list them all." Her attempted joke fell flat, but he didn't notice as he remembered he still had to slip out of her trailer without being seen.

"You're right, I do need to hurry. Thanks, darlin', for a good breakfast," he said as he picked up the last two biscuits and sliced them in half before putting pieces of sausage between the halves to make tiny sandwiches. After pulling on his heavy coat and dry but stiffened boots,

123

he leaned down for one last kiss. "And thanks for the best night of my life," he whispered as he tenderly stroked her cheek with his work-roughened palm.

"Encores are my specialty." She managed a shaky smile, wanting him to spend the next two nights with her, but she was too shy to come right out and ask him. It was important to her that he make the next overture.

"Some shows I never get tired of seeing over and over." He sensed her dilemma, but although he wanted her, he didn't want her to feel pushed or exploited, so he hesitated.

"I could save you a ticket," she offered timidly.

"In that case, I'll be there with bells on," he promised, a gentle smile softening his gray eyes before he moved to the front door.

CHAPTER NINE

"Sunny, come here quick!" Tyler called, a frantic note in his voice. "You've got to see this."

Sarah dropped the silverware into the sink with a crash and hurried to the doorway, wondering what could have Tyler so upset. Anxiously her eyes searched the scene in front of her.

"Look at that," he directed, excitement lighting up his handsome face. "Have you ever seen anything so beautiful?"

"I don't see anything special. Just some snow," Sarah answered, mystified by all the hullabaloo.

"Just snow!" he almost shouted. "Do you realize that the last time we had this much snow was in 1973? You are witnessing a big event."

She looked dubiously at the few inches of snow that barely covered the ground. It had been a long time since she had given snow a second thought, except when it spotted her boots or soaked through her pant legs. "There was two feet of dirty, sloppy snow in Denver last week when I left. What's so special about a few measly inches?"

"I don't think you are fully appreciating the magnitude of what you are seeing." He spoke patiently, as if to a slow child. "Around here we usually see a snowflake or two every year and maybe a thin layer of ice on the puddles, but it's usually too wet or warm for the flakes to stick. But when all of the conditions are just right and we get a heavy enough snowfall to actually see and touch, almost everyone takes the day off work or school and acts like a kid again."

"But there's not even enough to make a decent snowman," Sarah protested, still unable to share his enthusiasm.

"Of course there is. You'll be surprised by how many snowmen you'll see today. Sure, they might not be six feet tall with chunks of coal for eyes or derby hats, but the kids, young or old, that put them together have just as much fun as people up north who sculpt twenty-foot-tall ice statues."

Sarah found it was much more interesting to watch his animated face than to look out over the pathetic excuse for snow. Tyler's eyes were sparkling with childish delight. His thick dark hair fell across his forehead, adding to the boyish effect. She had a sneaking suspicion that despite his thirty-one years he wouldn't be able to restrain himself much longer from picking up a handful of snow and packing it neatly into a snowball to launch at some unsuspecting passerby.

"Hurry up and get dressed." He pushed her toward the bedroom. "You don't want to miss out on this, do you?" Expectantly he awaited her reaction.

Sarah sensed that this was some sort of impromptu test to gauge her reaction to something as ordinary as a snowfall. "No, of course I don't." She returned his relieved smile. "I haven't had a chance to enjoy snow since I was a kid. But you go ahead. I'm going to take a quick shower, and then I'll meet you near the campfire."

"Dress warmly. I don't want you to catch a cold," he cautioned before closing the door firmly behind him.

He was bringing her back to life, Sarah mused while the shower spray massaged her body. She had seen the scenery around her for the first time in years, just as she had really listened to what people were saying with newly opened ears. New or suppressed feelings were rushing through her, reminding her that she was a normal, healthy twenty-four-year-old woman who had been merely existing in an artificial world, surrounded by people who wouldn't recognize or appreciate honesty if it hit them in the face.

Unfortunately she was so deeply involved with her sister's career, with Sunny's single-minded drive for success, that she was not certain she could ever escape in spite of her own deep longings. After all, hadn't she proved she was just like everyone else when she agreed to go along with this deception? She hadn't really considered how many people, both directly and indirectly, would be affected by what had seemed like a harmless trick but had evolved into a complicated lie.

This was not the same thing as a movie stunt man's taking the place of the star for dangerous scenes. The public was never really deceived by that substitution because no attempt was ever made to conceal from the press or the public the fact that stunt men and stand-ins were being used. Everyone knew it was make-believe.

But last night had been real, and the cold, bright light of morning brought to mind the fact that unprotected sex sometimes resulted in unplanned children. Sarah loved children and wanted several of her own someday soon, but not *this* soon. If things were complicated now, they would be ten times worse if she had become pregnant during her one night of passion. As personally inexperienced as she was, she had nevertheless heard that stranger things had happened than that. A clear picture pushed its way into her imagination of an adorable child with dark tousled hair, gentle gray eyes, and round, rosy cheeks. Tyler would make a terrific father, she mused, then shrugged. Her common sense whispered that the sensible thing to do would be not to let things go as far as they had last night. But her new frivolous side begged her not to be so hasty. Maybe if there were a next time, Tyler would be prepared.

Such strange ideas were unusual for Sarah. Her main concern should be the successful completion of this week. A battle between desire and duty raged within her until her thoughts became more rational. At this point in the masquerade, in order to salvage Sunny's reputation and Sarah's self-respect, this scenario must be played to its natural conclusion. Any slipups or premature confessions would do more damage than good. When it was over, Sarah was determined to adopt Tyler's policy of never again letting herself get into a situation such as this one

128

regardless of the circumstances. For now, if she could keep it up for just two more days, then no one would be hurt—except maybe herself.

She took off her shower cap and combed the silken length of her hair before pulling it into a ponytail on top of her head and pinning it into a neat coil. She realized she should have brought along more than one wig. Although all of Sunny's wigs were made of an easy-care, natural-looking synthetic, Sarah just wasn't in the mood to waste the time it would take to restyle the forlorn creature that still hung on the towel bar in the bathroom. Instead she tied a scarf around her head to hide her own hair and put a cowboy hat firmly on top before leaving the trailer.

Thoughts of last night and the future were foremost in Tyler's mind as he went in search of Jed after feeding and watering the horses and changing into clean clothes. As usual Jed was at the campfire, distributing strong, hot coffee and doughnuts. When he saw Tyler, he headed for the chuck wagon to get out the breakfast supplies.

"Don't cook me any breakfast today, Jed," Tyler said as his long strides quickly caught up to the shorter man. "I've already eaten."

"How about Miss Day?" Jed asked with a knowing glance. "Will she be wanting anything this morning?"

"No, she cooked up some of the things you left in the camper." He was careful that no one else was within hearing distance as he answered.

129

"That was some storm we had last night, wasn't it?" Jed remarked.

"Yes, it was." Tyler nodded in agreement. "I just about froze to death until I got out of my wet clothes."

"Yeah, that wind was sure blowing hard," Jed persisted. "Sunny's trailer was really rocking when I stopped by, looking for you."

Tyler gave him a quick, sharp look. "Oh? What time was that?" he asked casually while furtively reassuring himself that no one else could hear this conversation.

"Oh, it was pretty late. I was a little worried about you when you didn't show up last night," Jed said with fatherly concern. "So I checked out a few of the places I thought you might be. Miss Day's trailer was the last place I looked, but no one answered my knock, so I gave up and went on back to the truck. I suppose you were okay, though."

"You shouldn't have worried. I was fine. I would have let you know where I was, but it was sort of a last-minute decision. I was drenched and cold, so she let me use her shower and then insisted I sleep on the sofa," he explained, avoiding the whole story.

"All I've got to say about that is you'd better remember that these Texas storms blow in fast and furious, wild and fierce while they last. But they don't last long, and in a few days the storm has been forgotten by everyone except those whose pipes froze and burst, flooding their houses with water."

"What are you trying to get at, Jed?" Tyler's eyes narrowed suspiciously. He had known this man all his life

130

and respected and trusted his opinions. Often his insight was eerie in its accuracy, and he didn't always say what Tyler wanted to hear.

"I've known men to have parts of their bodies froze plum off by a particularly ruthless storm," he teased, then added more seriously, "I just want you to be careful and not get hurt. You've got to remember that this is just temporary. When the cows start calving and the grass turns green, everything will be back like it was before you met her. You'd never be happy living in the eye of a hurricane, waiting for the winds to change."

"I know," Tyler said, a wistful note creeping into his voice. "Like I said before, none of this was planned, and I know I'll have to let go when she leaves. We have no middle ground on which to build a future. But thanks." He slapped the old man on the back affectionately.

"I'm just telling you what your father would say if he were still here," Jed muttered, trying to hide his emotions by rummaging through the grub box.

Tyler wandered back toward the campfire, trying to sort through his increasingly muddled thoughts. His own instincts had repeatedly echoed Jed's advice, and yet he couldn't stay away from Sunny Day. He was intelligent enough to weigh the pros against the cons and come up with a danger signal flashing its warning. Just two more days and the only time he would ever see her again would be at the rodeo or on TV. But it had to be enough because there could be no further commitment for either of them.

Unaware that Sarah's thoughts were paralleling his own, he was suddenly stopped in his tracks by the realization of what the consequences of last night's rashness might be. Since Sunny had been a virgin and could not possibly have anticipated how the evening would end, it was unlikely that she had used any form of birth control. He had felt the loss of a child once before, even though it had turned out that it had not been his. Since then he had been scrupulously careful that such a situation would not recur—until last night. It was another example of how much she affected him. He had to remain in control of himself or he could live to regret it.

The bright turquoise scarf tails that closely matched the heavily brocaded western-style blouse Sarah was wearing lay against her cheek like the petals of an exotic flower, bringing out the greenish tint of her eyes. It was fortunate her coat had been intended for use up north, where it was so often very cold and wet, because she would need its extra protection today.

There was quite a lot of activity around the campsite as people made their preparations for the day's ride or, as Tyler had predicted, frolicked like children in the snow. Already bare patches of ground showed through the white covering as the traffic and scuffling redistributed the thin layer of snow. The sun pierced weakly through the patchy clouds, adding a fresh sparkle to the scene. There was a beauty and innocence to the snow-covered setting that Sarah observed with euphoric eyes. Common things that she hadn't even noticed yesterday had been transformed into shimmering ornaments. Skeletal branches were dotted with diamond teardrops, tall dried grass had frozen into shrouded spikes, and windswept pine needles were stiffened, as if the icy blast were still blowing against them. Long dramatic icicles hung from everything like fairy stalactites in a crystal cave. Touched by winter's icy hand, the Texas landscape had been changed into a glistening work of art.

The whole world was more beautiful today than it had been yesterday or last week or last year. She was no longer the same person she had been then, and it was not just because she was pretending to be Sunny. It was because she was happily, at least for the next forty-eight hours, enjoying the discovery of herself as a woman. Surely no other female felt as special and satisfied as she did today. There was a new awareness of her own individuality, even though at the moment she was a person with too many names and too few answers.

Tyler joined her as soon as he saw her leave the trailer. His cheeks were flushed a bright red, and his eyes still sparkled mischievously. Sarah noticed the scattered remains of several snowballs still clinging to the sheepskin collar and buckskin hide of his heavy coat.

"You've obviously been busy while I was dressing," she commented with a twinkle. "Who won?"

"I did, of course. I'm the boss," he said, laughing. "My men treat me with the greatest respect and—" Abruptly his boast was cut off as a snowball hit him solidly on the back of his head, knocking his hat off and sending a chilling trickle of frozen flakes down his collar.

"I can certainly see that they do." Her eyebrows arched in amusement as she nodded wryly, which earned

133

her a reproachful glare from Tyler as he bent to pick up his hat. It was difficult, however, to take this man's gruff look seriously while his rumpled black hair dripped with melting snow and the corners of his mouth twitched suspiciously.

"If there weren't so many camera crews or curious eyes around right now, I'd show you that our Texas snow is just as good as any snow for having a snowball fight," he threatened with a playful snarl.

"Hah! I was the fastest, most accurate snowball thrower in Fayette County. I'm afraid you wouldn't get any respect from me either." She flashed back a grin.

"I knew you wouldn't respect me if I let you have your way with me last night." He lowered his voice so only she could hear his pretended remorse. "Men need respect, too, you know."

"That's the price you have to pay for your actions," she retaliated in the same bantering tone. "You had heard that I couldn't resist gorgeous men dressed only in blue bath towels. So now your reputation is hopelessly ruined."

"Since it's already ruined, why don't we go back to the trailer and catch up with the others tomorrow?" he joked with a suggestive wink.

She responded with a burst of laughter and a decidedly disrespectful "You're hopeless." A news team was approaching, and they had to return to their roles, but during the interview, whenever their eyes met, a silent communication flashed between them.

As much as she wanted to ride with Tyler today, Sarah

felt it would not be in character for Sunny to risk catching a cold and damaging her voice. So, reluctantly she rode in the cab of the truck with Jed. It wasn't that she didn't like Jed, although she suspected that he wasn't overly fond of her; it was just that she hated to waste even one precious hour that could have been spent with Tyler. She watched without enthusiasm as the trail riders set out.

The group was somewhat smaller today because the younger children and their mothers, along with a few of the less dedicated, had given up and gone home early. But later today the Salt Grass Trail Ride would merge with the Valley Lodge Trail Ride, which would increase the total number of riders by several hundred. It would also mean there would be a whole new group of fans to meet and autographs to sign tonight, but this was a chore that Sarah was becoming accustomed to. She still couldn't understand how Sunny could put up with being constantly in the public eye the way she was. The truth was that Sunny not only put up with it but loved almost every minute of it. Sarah, on the other hand, couldn't wait for the return of her anonymity and privacy.

Today Sarah was going to witness the behind-the-scenes operations that kept the trail ride going. After the riders left each morning, the people left behind had to break camp, hook up the trailers, and clean up the mess so that the Texas landscape didn't suffer from having had so large a group spend the night there. The caravan then moved to the preplanned meeting point for lunch, where they stopped and prepared the noon meal so it would be ready when the riders arrived. This procedure was repeated as the trucks, campers, horse trailers, and vans again passed the long line of riders before stopping and setting up camp at that night's scheduled stopping place.

The riders, after spending many long hours in the saddle, were grateful they didn't have the dismal chore of setting up camp to look forward to at the end of each day. But still, most of them never realized how much work and planning it took to coordinate such a massive effort.

Sarah gained new respect for the people who had come along on the trail ride not to party and have a good time but to spend long hours laboring to make sure all the others enjoyed themselves. But she could not resist a look of longing as they passed the riders making their way carefully along the sometimes icy highway. Today they were traveling down Interstate 10 with a police escort blocking off traffic on one of the three eastbound lanes so the trail ride could continue in safety. A horse and rider could travel at a steady pace of from five to seven miles an hour. But with this many people, horses, mules, and wagons involved, the trail riders barely covered three miles an hour. And today, because of the unusually slippery conditions, it would take them even longer.

Sarah watched without interest as she and Jed passed mile after mile of flat, empty fields with their glistening white winter coat. Small clusters of businesses hugged the highway at distant intervals, but most of them appeared to be deserted today.

At the lunch break Tyler explained that the Gulf Coast

136

area of Texas became almost completely paralyzed during the few days of ice and snow that they might experience every couple of years. No one down here was equipped to deal with this type of weather, and except for the transplanted northerners no one knew how to drive under these conditions.

"It's too bad you won't still be here in the springtime. You can't imagine how beautiful this part of Texas is when the wild flowers are in bloom. From here to the hill country there will be thousands of acres covered with bright scarlet Indian paintbrushes, purplish bluebonnets, delicate yellow buttercups, and small golden daisylike flowers," Tyler said between bites of his hamburger. "You should make it a point to swing back through here in April or early May if you can work it into your schedule."

He was obviously proud of his home state, but his words only served as an unpleasant reminder to Sarah that she wouldn't be here in April to see Texas in bloom, or more importantly, to see Tyler. And he hadn't even hinted that he wanted her to stay or that he wanted to be the one to show her the springtime display. Sarah spent the remainder of the afternoon trying to hide the ache that gripped her heart. It proved to be the greatest challenge she had been faced with so far this week.

"Do you work at Tyler's ranch, Jed?" she asked her silent companion as they traveled from the spot where they'd stopped for lunch to that night's campground.

"No, I'm just an old friend of the family."

"Oh, so you're not their cook back home?"

Her question brought the first genuine grin to his face that she had seen all week. "No, I only cook when Tyler drags me along on these trail rides. I learned how to cook for large groups in the army and never could scale it down after I got home. So this is my once-a-year chance to show my stuff and keep in practice."

"You're very good. Maybe you should open a restaurant. I'll bet it would do well," she suggested.

"I stay pretty busy at my job." He chuckled before adding, "I suppose Tyler hasn't told you that I'm the president of his bank."

"You're joking." Sarah tried to disguise her shock. "Why would a bank president spend a week cooking and taking care of all these men?"

"Because I enjoy it," he stated simply. "As you can imagine, it's quite a change from what I do the rest of the year. I'm too old and out of shape to ride on a horse, but I love getting outdoors and being just one of the guys."

"Well, I wish Tyler had told me so I wouldn't have asked you all those stupid questions." Her flushed cheeks showed her embarrassment. She had just assumed this roughly dressed, soft-spoken man was one of Tyler's ranch hands. It was difficult to envision him dressed in a three-piece suit and sitting behind a big wooden desk instead of standing beside the huge cast-iron pot hanging over an open fire, stirring a batch of spicy chili.

"Tyler probably never gives my title a second thought. He's not one to attach any importance to things like that. Either he likes you for who you really are, or he doesn't.

138

He can spot a phony a mile away; a big fancy title doesn't make any difference to him."

Luckily they were turning into Bear Creek Park, because Sarah had suddenly become speechless. She had taken Jed's words very personally. Maybe she was getting paranoid or experiencing a fresh wave of guilt, but it seemed that every finger was pointed at her and every whisper was about her. But it was impossible for anyone to know her secret. She had not slipped or let her guard down except in front of Tyler, and she could trust him, couldn't she?

To keep her mind off these troublesome thoughts, she puttered around camp, watching the activity and pitching in to help Jed prepare supper. She peeled mounds of potatoes, which he sliced into long, thick french fries. Several blackened cast-iron skillets sizzled and spit as Jed dropped the breaded pieces of chicken into the hot oil. Sarah kept glancing at her watch, wondering how much longer it would be before the riders made it into camp.

It was almost dark before she saw the flashing lights of the patrol car that was escorting the riders and heard the familiar sounds of harnesses jingling and hooves clattering on the pavement. As if he, too, had resented the separation, Tyler was one of the first riders to enter the circle of campers.

With a forced casualness Sarah leaned back against the camper as he dismounted from his horse. What she wanted to do was to rush over to him, throw her arms around his neck, and kiss the warmth back into his cold face.

"Hi, darlin'." His smooth baritone wrapped around her like a velvet blanket, sending delightful shivers skittering through her. "Did you miss me?"

"What an ego!" she snorted, refusing to let him know just how much she had missed him today. "Have you ever considered a career in show business?"

"I'd hate it," he retorted sharply, suddenly serious. Then at the hurt expression that stole away her smile, he added more gently, "Why don't you keep me company while I feed the horses? We've got a whole new group of people tonight, and as soon as they discover you, we probably won't have a minute alone."

She brightened at this indication that he enjoyed being with her, and she eagerly went with him to the horse trailer where he kept the horses' food and supplies. Zena nickered a greeting, glad to see them after a lonely day spent in the horse trailer. Tyler backed her out and tied her next to his gelding. Sarah sat on a flat-topped stump and watched him as he unsaddled his horse and groomed both horses. It was such a simple pleasure to be able to look at him, admiring his lean, muscular build. Even though it was partially hidden by his bulky coat, it held no mysteries for her after last night, and a picture of his magnificent nude body flashed through her mind.

"I'll up my ante to five dollars for your thoughts," he teased with a knowing grin. "They look like they're worth at least that much if the color of your cheeks is any indication."

His observation caused her to blush even redder, but

140

she managed to mumble, "I was just admiring your coat."

"Sure you were," he agreed dryly. "And I've been meaning to tell you how much I've been thinking about yours. Maybe later we can compare tailors . . . or something," he finished with a suggestive wink that left no doubt as to his meaning.

"I should be able to ride again tomorrow. The weather report said it would warm up into the fifties." She looked around her regretfully as she said, "But it looks like all of your snow will soon be gone." The afternoon sun had taken its toll, leaving drifts only in shadowed or sheltered areas. By the following day, soon after daylight, the last flake would have melted away.

"Nothing lasts forever, does it?" He glanced pensively over his gelding's broad back, memorizing each perfect feature of her beautiful face.

"No, I guess it doesn't," she agreed, equally wistful. It was foolish of her to even dream of a happily-ever-after ending to this relationship. The best she could hope for was a "Thanks for the memory." Restlessly she jumped to her feet and said, "Supper has been ready for half an hour. Jed will skin us alive if we don't hurry up and eat."

Tyler fastened the hobbles on the horses' front legs. "I sure don't want to get Jed mad at me. One of the unbreakable rules of the trail is not, under any circumstances, to upset the cook. I can finish settling the horses later."

As they walked back to camp Sarah said, "Why didn't you tell me who Jed was? I had a bad case of foot-in-mouth disease today when I asked him if he was your full-time cook. And then I even told him he should open a restaurant," she related, still upset by her faux pas.

"I'll bet he got a kick out of that," Tyler hooted, unsympathetic to her discomfort. "You probably wouldn't know it by looking at him, but he's one of the most intelligent men I've ever met. He started out as a teller and now has a controlling interest in the bank. But it's his cooking that he's most sensitive about. You could compliment him on anything else and not get much of a response, but if you told him you liked his cooking, you've probably made a friend for life."

"Yeah, all it took was one compliment and peeling six hundred thousand potatoes," she joked, adding a dramatic moan for effect.

"That should do it, all right," Tyler agreed, looking down on her fondly. "You've got everyone eating out of your hand."

"And you complained about paper plates!" she shot back, her eyes dancing in the firelight as they approached the chuck wagon.

As expected, they had barely filled their plates and sat down at one of the folding tables when people started sidling up to Sarah. It was a replay of what had happened earlier in the week, and she took it all in stride. Her food got cold, and still there was one more album to autograph or one more picture to sign. The night before, when they were in town, several of the original riders had purchased fan magazines that had Sunny's face plastered from cover to cover. Sarah didn't take the time to read the articles, which appeared to contain the usual speculations about who was Sunny's latest conquest. She played her role perfectly, coquettishly refusing to name any names or admit to any dalliances but tossing out enough noninformation to keep everyone guessing.

Suddenly someone thrust a magazine in front of her face with a particularly unflattering picture of Sunny leaning heavily against an unidentified man, as if she were either very drunk or very sick. The headlines jumped out at Sarah, causing her stomach to tighten in fear as she quickly read, "TOO MUCH BOOZE AND TOO LITTLE TALENT PUSH SUNNY DAY INTO A COMPLETE NERVOUS BREAKDOWN."

CHAPTER TEN

Shocked, Sarah scanned the article, picking out key phrases such as "wild erratic behavior," "inconsistent quality," "a has-been at twenty-four," "unstable and irresponsible," "too many late nights," and "numerous performances canceled at the last minute make her a bad risk." Had something awful happened to Sunny after they had parted last weekend? Had Sarah been so out of touch that she hadn't known that Sunny was lying in a hospital room right now? Her hands were shaking as she checked the date on the magazine's cover.

It was two months old. Not only was the magazine out of date, but the author had dug up a few of Sunny's past mistakes and expanded them into a slanderous character assassination. Sarah's fear turned into a fierce, protective anger. Some of the accusations were partially true, but that didn't give anyone the right to pass judgment on Sunny. She was trying to straighten out her life, and this magazine had no right printing this damaging trumped-up story.

"These are filthy lies," she snapped as she pushed abruptly away from the table. "You shouldn't waste your money on trash like this." And with a flick of her wrist she tossed the magazine into the campfire. "If you will remind me tomorrow, I've got some autographed pictures in the trailer that I'd be happy to give you," she said to the astonished owner of the magazine that was now being greedily consumed by the flames. "If you will excuse me, I'm going to my camper." Stiffly, her hands clenched into fists, she stalked away from the dumb-struck group.

She knew she shouldn't let some glory-seeking author upset her like this, but no one else realized how hard Sunny worked or how difficult the life of an entertainer was. Possibly it wouldn't be so bad if Sunny had achieved the status of Dolly Parton or Loretta Lynn. But even these big-time stars spent much of each year performing on the road. And no matter how famous you got, you never stopped being a target for every vicious reporter who didn't have anything better to write about. In fact, it seemed like the bigger you got, the bigger the lies that were printed about you.

The publicity about Sunny's questionable love life usually contained only a small percentage of truth, but the public expected and applauded outrageous behavior. These stories could be ignored or encouraged, depending on what kind of coverage Sunny needed at the time. But when doubts were cast on her mental stability or her professional ability, important people began to pay attention. These were the people who set up the bookings and negotiated the contracts. There was a big difference between singing at a major rodeo and singing at a high school prom. It had taken Sunny too many years of hard work to pull herself up to where she was today for a few half-truths and cruel accusations to send it all crashing down around her.

Sarah wondered if Mack had seen this article. He probably had, or he wouldn't have come down so hard on Sunny for trying to back out of her commitment to appear on this trail ride and in Houston. Mack was an excellent manager, always arranging for Sunny to get top dollar for her shows. And he really did have her best interests at heart, never finalizing a booking until Sunny gave her approval.

The whole problem was that Sunny didn't realize that being young and beautiful with more than her share of talent did not mean that her career couldn't be ruined by her careless behavior. She must learn to discipline herself if she intended to stay in this business for a long time.

Helpless tears rolled down Sarah's cheeks. She longed for the comfort and strength of Tyler's arms, but he was one of the reasons she was crying. Even though there was a basis in truth for several of the accusations about Sunny, it was imperative that no one else know that. Sunny's career could not survive the blow, and for Sunny her career was her life. Sarah would do anything in her power to help Sunny, and that included sacrificing her relationship with Tyler if there was even a remote possibility that he would become infuriated at her admission and tell the press. It would be like throwing Sunny to the wolves.

Sarah showered and dressed for bed. She didn't know

if Tyler would stop by to see her after everyone else left the area. More importantly, she didn't know if she wanted him to. Despondently she sat in her darkened trailer, listening to the shouts of laughter and bursts of song from the other riders. Still sitting on the sofa, her feet tucked under the full skirt of her gown, she fell into an exhausted sleep.

A muffled knock woke her, and she glanced at her watch. Even without seeing the time she knew from the quiet outside that it must be fairly late. Rubbing and stretching a crick in her neck, she reached for a light switch.

"It's me, Tyler. Are you okay?" he whispered loudly.

With a relieved sigh she opened the door. Regardless of how she should feel, she was glad that he was here. "Come in," she invited, suddenly shy as she saw him standing on her doorstep, his hat held in his hands and his face boyishly handsome in the soft moonlight.

"I didn't know whether to come by tonight or not." His normally self-assured voice held a note of uncertainty. "You were so upset that I thought you might need to talk to someone."

"Not just someone," she said softly as she shut the door behind him. "I need you." For several seconds they stood apart, neither speaking as their eyes feasted on each other. It had been a long hard day, made worse by their separation, and although neither appeared to make the first move, they were suddenly in each other's arms.

Carelessly he tossed his hat on the sofa, following it up with his heavy coat. Eagerly he crushed her slim warm body against him, his hands savoring the stimulating sensation of slick silk sliding over her smooth, soft skin. Her feminine figure snuggled next to him, fitting perfectly against his hardened male physique. Sensing her need to be comforted, he just held her tightly, crooning gentle words of consolation while she clung to him.

"You didn't believe any of those lies, did you?" she murmured anxiously, tilting her head back so she could see his expression.

"Of course not," he was quick to reassure her. "The person I've gotten to know in the last few days bears no resemblance to the person in that article. You're one of the most decent, kindhearted ladies I've ever had the pleasure to meet. I have no questions about your sanity or stability."

"I never feel very sane when I'm in your arms," she breathed against his approaching lips, unable to worry about Sunny's problems when she could feel the accelerated thumping of his heart against her breast.

"You've been driving me crazy too," he answered as he tenderly took possession of her mouth before showering her eyes, forehead, cheeks, and even the tip of her small nose with ardent kisses.

"Do you want me to stop?" she asked, pulling the tails of his shirt out of his pants with seductive slowness. It pleased her to know that she drove him beyond reason, because he had the same disturbing effect on her. When he held her, she lost all awareness of time or place; of right and wrong.

"No," he returned to the intoxicating sweetness of her

lips. "I just want you to make it a short trip." His hands eased the gown off her shoulders, helping it glide down the long line of her body to lie in a shiny puddle of fabric on the carpet.

Her own eager fingers pulled apart the line of snaps that ran down the front of his shirt before sliding around to stroke the taut muscles of his broad shoulders. She shuddered in delight as his hand found one breast, kneading it gently as he cradled it in his work-roughened palm.

Desire raced through her body like fire, melting her bones until she leaned limply against him. He hugged her tightly, possessively while his lips became more demanding.

His voice deepened hoarsely as he asked, "Are we going to fight over the sofa and the bed again tonight?"

"I'm a lover, not a fighter." She smiled coquettishly. "Forget the sofa! I'll race you to the bed."

"Oh, no, you won't. I'm not letting go of you until daylight," he promised, lifting her easily and carrying her into the bedroom.

As she lay back against the pillows she watched him shed his clothes with surprising speed, the classic beauty of his rippling muscles and tapered masculine build filling her with a pulsing warmth that could be satisfied only by him.

Returning the compliment, his eyes studied her as if trying to memorize every lovely inch of her body. She could feel the caress of his eyes as vividly as if he were stroking her with his hands. Their gray softness followed her graceful curves from the top of her firm full breasts down into the shadowy valley of her femininity. Restlessly she writhed beneath his gaze in a primitive plea for relief from the building tension as he prepared for their lovemaking. She looked at him with gratitude shining in her eyes for his thoughtfulness in wanting to protect her.

"God, you're incredible," he murmured as his body covered hers, his flesh throbbing against her softness. The driving passion of his kiss parted her lips, allowing him access to plunder the moist sweetness of her mouth. His hands touched and teased, tuning her body as tightly as the strings of a guitar until they came together in nature's perfect harmony. Their symphony climbed to a frenzied crescendo, then faded slowly into a gentle lullaby.

A languor born of complete contentment kept them entwined together for several quiet minutes after their passions had been temporarily sated. At last Tyler spoke, his words muffled by her cloud of hair, which pillowed his head.

"I don't see why you were so worried about those lies in that magazine article," he commented huskily. "Last night you proved to me that I shouldn't believe everything I read about you."

"What do you mean?" She shifted slightly so she could see his face, which rested only inches from hers.

"I meant that after everything I had heard about your active sex life, you can imagine my surprise when I found out the truth."

"Oh, that," she muttered, a pink flush staining her cheeks as she tried to think of a believable explanation.

"It isn't exactly a subject you want debated by the press," she hedged.

"Well, as soon as I get home, I'm going to cancel all my magazine subscriptions," he teased before adding seriously, "but I'm glad I was the one to find out the truth."

This conversation was entirely too personal and becoming more dangerous by the moment. It was peculiar how her own lack of experience and Sunny's unjustly publicized overabundance of it had chosen this moment to surface. Embarrassed and unsure of how she should react to this touchy situation, Sarah turned away from him.

"Hey, I didn't mean to embarrass you," he soothed. "I'm proud to be your first lover, and I'm sorry I brought the subject up at all. It was just that everything about you is so different from the way I thought it would be."

Sarah caught her breath in alarm. She knew she had let her emotions carry her too far. She had always prided herself on her self-control, but that was before she had met Tyler. There was an animal magnetism between them that she was helpless to resist. But, she comforted herself, as long as he never learned the whole truth, how could she possibly regret this time spent in his arms?

"Don't get me wrong," he hastened to add. "The surprises have all been terrific. I think I'll volunteer for this job every year." Laughing, he dodged her playful punch, which landed harmlessly against the rock-hard muscle of his bicep.

"I hope they get Willie Nelson next year," she retorted

with an innocent flutter of her thick, dark eyelashes. "His hair is almost as long as mine."

"Somehow I don't think it would be as much fun," he teased as he leaned over her, one hand tracing the graceful curve of her jaw. "Speaking of Willie Nelson, have you ever noticed how many country and western singers have names that end with that *ee* sound? Is it some sort of unwritten rule that to be successful, you must be named Johnny, Charlie, Kenny, Mickey, or Bobby?" he commented with an engaging grin.

"Only if you're a man," she responded with amusement, then continued, "No, I had never really noticed it before. I guess it makes them sound more friendly and down-to-earth, like good old boys."

"How about you? Is Sunny your real name, or did you change it for your career?" His fingers trailed along her cheekbone and circled her small ear before burying themselves in the rich thickness of her silken hair.

For just a moment Sarah hesitated. She was tempted to tell him her real name. Apparently he didn't pay enough attention to the fan magazines to know that Sunny had a twin sister named Sarah. The fact that Mack had never thought it wise to play up their relationship had come in handy this week, but could she get by with telling Tyler that her name was Sarah? It was sort of a silly desire, but just once she longed to hear her name whispered from his lips in the same warm, caressing tone that he used when he called her Sunny.

There is nothing so personal and intimate as a person's own name. She somehow felt that when she had left her

152

name behind, she had lost an important part of her identity. But she was not Sarah, she repeated to herself, she was Sunny. And as Sunny she responded, "My real name is Sandra Dayton. I changed the Dayton to Day when I started singing professionally, but everyone has called me Sunny for as long as I can remember. They told me it had to do with my bright, sparkling personality," she joked to hide her distress.

"And what did they say about your humility?" he teased with dry humor.

"They told me that famous people don't need humility. In fact, it's a liability. It makes a person susceptible to being hurt by unconstructive criticism."

"And now it's my turn to make a deep dark confession," he remarked, his expression suddenly serious.

Her heart fluttered wildly. He *did* suspect something. It was all over. Because of one—no, make that two glorious nights, her weakness had ruined Sunny's career. Sarah would never be able to make this up to Sunny. She continued to berate herself while waiting for the ax to fall. His next words could not have been more unexpected or welcome in their innocence.

"I hate to admit this to you," he paused, trying not to sound unkind, "but I like rock and roll."

"What?" she exclaimed as she went limp with relief.

"I love to hear you sing, but I've just never been what you might call a die-hard country and western music fan. I don't even own a Hank Williams record or have one of my radio pushbuttons tuned to a country station," he confessed somewhat sheepishly.

153

"I just can't believe it," she replied, still referring to the fact that he wasn't going to expose her fakery.

But he misunderstood and thought she was genuinely upset because he wasn't properly appreciative of her career. "It's just that I grew up listening to the Beatles and the Beach Boys. Back then country wasn't cool." He grinned, trying to coax her back into a good mood.

"Don't feel bad," she answered and, to his surprise, laughed merrily. "Not only do I love those two groups, but some of the more recent rock-and-roll imports such as Adam Ant and Men At Work are particular favorites of mine. I've always agreed that variety is the spice of life."

"I'm completely satisfied with just you, right here, right now." Tyler's breath was hot against her neck as he nibbled his way down to one of her pink nipples. "You sing like a bird, look like an angel, and make love like a tigress," he whispered seductively, pulling the rosy peak into his greedy mouth.

"You're going to be exhausted in the morning," she protested halfheartedly. "We haven't gotten much sleep during the last two nights."

"How can I get any rest with you here next to me?" he asked, then let his darting tongue rekindle the flame of desire. "I can get all the sleep I need next week, when you're gone."

He spoke so softly that she had to strain to hear him, but as the full impact of his words struck her a lump rose in her throat. He had crushed whatever small impractical hopes she might have had about their future together. It

154

was clear that he was not expecting any more from this relationship than what they shared here in this trailer. But, she realized with a piercing constriction in her chest that made breathing extremely difficult, he had taken possession of more than just her body; he now owned her heart.

That she was so strongly attracted to him and that they had shared so much in such a short time did not change the fact that they would probably never see each other again after Saturday. It was no longer a question of whether or not she would miss him but of how much.

Fiercely her fingers dug into his back, pulling him closer. With so little time left she must take advantage of every second. Maybe then she wouldn't have time to think of the lonely hours . . . weeks . . . years she had ahead of her.

The weather cooperated, and Sarah was able to ride with the others on the last day of the trail ride. It seemed incredible that the weather could change so dramatically in such a short time. Today the temperature rose into the low sixties.

Again this morning the trail ride officials had arrived to make their daily inspection. It was their job to visit each trail ride once a day to make sure that everyone was abiding by the rules, so as to keep the trail rides up to the standards of the Houston Livestock Show and Rodeo Association. They checked to make sure that the animals were receiving the proper treatment, even going so far as to count the number of people in the wagons to be certain that the loads weren't too heavy for the teams. Also they judged each trail ride on its authenticity, marking down anyone who wore tennis shoes, T-shirts, or baseball caps, rode double on the horses, or was seen with an open beer can in hand. All this scrutiny encouraged the trail riders to perpetuate the image of the trail ride as a wholesome family event set in an Old West atmosphere. It was all part of the fun, and everyone cooperated, hoping their trail ride would be awarded the coveted yearly prize.

Because Tyler was the chairman of the Trail Ride Committee he normally would have accompanied these men on their daily rounds. But since this was the first year that a celebrity of greater fame than a member of a local television news team or a radio station DJ had accepted the invitation to join the trail ride, he had agreed to the added responsibility of taking care of this star. As he had told Sarah earlier, he had not been looking forward to this new duty, but because he, too, knew the value of good publicity—in this case, for the Livestock Show and Rodeo—he had overcome his reservations.

Each year Tyler volunteered to donate his time to this worthy cause. Not only was the show the finest entertainment event anywhere in the Southwest with its championship rodeo, livestock exhibitions, and wide variety of other competitions, but the Livestock Show and Rodeo Association was the largest donor of agricultural scholarships in the nation. As a nonprofit charitable organization, the association was dedicated to the support of young people, education, and agricultural research.

The trail riders set out on this, the last leg of their

journey, with renewed enthusiasm and raised spirits. Although they were already within the Houston city limits, they were still at least ten miles from their final destination. Because of the complicated freeway system and the heavy traffic, today's ride was the most difficult and dangerous part of the entire journey. Most vehicles sped past, bathing the riders in fumes and noise, which had almost been forgotten during the past few days filled with fresh country air and rural quiet. But some drivers slowed down, enjoying the unusual sight of horses and wagons that belonged in another century. Commuters called greetings, waving and whistling as they searched for Sunny Day among the hundreds of riders.

Most of those who looked were rewarded with at least a glimpse of a slim, sexy body that they assumed was her, sitting with grace and ease on the back of a beautiful horse. Sarah was playing her role to the hilt. Her dazzling outfit, fashioned out of soft leather as snowy white as Zena and studded with hundreds of sparkling rhinestones, set her apart from the others in the scruffy, travel-worn group.

It had been a real struggle for her to pull it all together this morning. She and Tyler had talked and loved through most of the night, just catnapping in each other's arms. Reluctantly he had left her early, before anyone else was awake. As tired as she was, she had been unable to sleep without the warmth and security of his strong arms, so she had used the extra time to restyle Sunny's wig and select an outfit from her garment bag that would be both warm and stunning.

157

As Tyler kept a personal as well as professional eye on her, he couldn't help thinking that as devastatingly attractive as she looked today, the picture that would remain forever engraved in his memory was the way she had looked this morning just before dawn. Sitting in the middle of the rumpled bed, her enticingly nude figure swathed in a swirl of sheets, she had looked so fragile and vulnerable that he had had to reach deep into his reserve of willpower to force himself to leave her then. Her full swollen lips had begged to be kissed, and her sleepy heavy-lidded eyes had called him back to bed, while the rosy tips of her breasts peaked invitingly through the tumble of golden curls that had fallen around her shoulders like a spill of sunlight in the dimly lit room.

Only the fact that he knew he would be seeing her again soon had propelled him from the trailer into the cool darkness of the early morning. But he didn't know what could force him to leave her on Saturday after the parade, when there would be no promises that they would ever be together again. No promises unless he was willing to compromise his life-style and let her continue her career. It wasn't that he objected to having a working wife; it was just that in Sunny's line of work she would be away from home more often than she'd be at home, and Tyler didn't know if he could accept that. It just wasn't the life he had planned for himself and his future family.

Living in the public eye was very inhibiting and uncomfortable. This week had clearly illustrated that a celebrity's world was filled with constant attention and excitement and allowed very limited privacy. Although it

158

didn't appear to have done any permanent harm to Sunny's warm, natural personality, there was no guarantee that it wouldn't some day overwhelm her—and him.

For Tyler and Sarah the day was filled with bittersweet thoughts and tender looks. But it was much too short. There had been no opportunity for private conversation. Overreacting to the noise of the traffic, the horses had required extra attention to keep them under control. Although well trained and tired from the last four days, they had been fidgety and nervous, as if they had known they were nearing the last campsite and were eager to get there. The riders, too, had been even more boisterous than usual, and it was carrying over into the evening hours.

The Salt Grass Trail Ride entered Memorial Park around five o'clock. Several other trail rides were already there, setting up camp for the night and getting ready for the evening's festivities. Every year on the last night before the big parade, all the trail rides converged at Memorial Park for one last party. And what a party it was! It started with a full-scale Texas barbecue, complete with all the trimmings. After supper there would be a dance that would last into the wee hours of the morning.

Thousands of riders, horses, mules, and other livestock spread out under the huge trees. Now that the weather had improved, families were reunited, ready to ride together in the big parade tomorrow morning. Hundreds of campers and horse trailers made the parking areas look like a recreational vehicle exhibition. The media, too, were out in full force, taking pictures, doing spontaneous interviews, and sampling the food.

Sarah showered and dressed with extra care. She didn't have much hope of being alone with Tyler until after the dance, but she wanted to look so nice that he wouldn't be able to think of anything else until they were together. They had one last night, and she intended to make it count.

Tyler's smoky gray eyes told her she had succeeded in capturing his undivided attention as she left the trailer.

"That's some outfit," he commented, his voice warm with admiration. "What color would you call that?"

"Blue," she stated simply, then laughed at his exasperated expression.

"I know it's blue, but what about all of those other colors in there. It changes every time you move."

"I'm not sure what it's real name is, but it looks sort of iridescent. I guess it was made for people who couldn't decide what color they wanted to wear."

"You look like a star." He reached out and ran his finger lightly down her shiny sleeve, leaving a rainbow trail that sent sparks shooting all through her body. Whenever she was near him, it seemed that all her sensitive nerve endings were exposed to the air, making her tingle with a sort of pleasurable pain.

"I am a star," she teased, trying to keep the conversation light.

"Not that kind of star," he snorted. "I meant a heavenly star, you know, as in 'Star light, star bright, first star I see tonight . . .' "

" 'Wish I may, wish I might . . .' " she broke in softly.

" 'Have my wish come true tonight,' " they finished together, their eyes betraying the secret wishes of their hearts.

"How would you like to go to a wedding?" he asked with a grin.

She stared at him suspiciously. "A wedding? Whose?"

"Actually we have our choice. There are three or four ceremonies that will be taking place before supper."

"You mean people from the trail rides are getting married right here and now?"

"Sure, why not? These long days and nights of togetherness do have a way of bringing people closer," he said as his dark eyebrows arched expressively. "But, on the other hand, I'm sure several new divorces will be filed next week because of the unacceptable extracurricular activities of some of the riders."

"I've never believed in love at first sight," she said skeptically. "Don't you think knowing someone just a week is rushing it a little?" She watched his face carefully. His answer was very important to her.

"I guess it's sort of like believing in UFO's," he replied with a thoughtful smile. "Until it happens to you, you never can be absolutely sure, can you?" Then with a shrug of his broad shoulders he added, "But in the case of most of these weddings it was lust at first sight. People just sort of get caught up in all the excitement and take their romances a little too seriously. Most of them won't last until next year's trail ride."

161

Even though he had been talking about other people, his meaning had come through to her loud and clear. He was as much as telling her that their relationship, while undeniably sweet, would also be short. This clarification of his intentions should have relieved her fears about possible future repercussions, but for some reason she felt let down. "Why would they do it if the odds are so badly stacked against them?"

"I suppose everyone has at one time or another been a blindly optimistic romantic."

"Even you?"

"Sure. Even me." He grinned, almost sheepishly. "Besides, not all of these marriages end in divorce court. Some last until that great roundup in the sky. I've heard of people who have met on a trail ride or somewhere a little more normal and then decided it would be fun to tie the knot out here on the prairie in front of God, their friends, and their horses—and who never once considered divorce."

"When you put it that way, I suppose it does sound romantic," she agreed. "Okay, then. Let's go to a wedding. But am I dressed properly for this uncivil ceremony?" she asked, the twinkle returning to her eyes.

"At weddings like these you can't go wrong. If anything, you might even be a little overdressed." Then as he wrapped his arm loosely but possessively around her slim waist, he bent to whisper in her ear, "The public has never seen you look your best, and as long as I'm around they never will!"

The warm tickle of his breath against her skin sent

162

shivers of delight through her veins. Hopeless romantic or not, under different circumstances it would not have been difficult to let herself fall in love with this man. But he would never know, and neither would she, how well they would suit each other. As with most of the other newly matched couples on this trail ride, the odds would be against them.

Together Sarah and Tyler strolled over to the site of one of the wedding ceremonies. The bride and groom were suitably attired in dress shirts, jeans that were partially covered by leather chaps, and cowboy hats decorated with flowers on hers and one tall turkey feather on his. The bridesmaids and groomsmen were similarly dressed, and all the members of the wedding party were on horseback, with the exception of the preacher, who stood on an overturned wooden crate.

After the vows the bride fumbled with a blue garter that had been hidden beneath her chaps, struggling to stretch it over her cowboy boots before flinging it into the crowd. A determined cowboy several feet in front of Tyler and Sarah caught it in midair as his friends cheered and hooted, and his girlfriend looked on in obvious delight.

"They should have played 'Happy Trails to You' instead of the 'Wedding March,' " Tyler whispered irreverently in her ear, returning the smile to her lips.

"There she is now. Oh, Miss Day, would you mind having your picture taken with Buford?" a man asked as he approached her with a portable television camera balanced on his shoulder.

163

"Of course not. Who is Buford?" she asked politely, looking around her for the mystery man.

"This is Buford," another man said as he led a very large, very fierce-looking Brahma bull toward her. At her sudden expression of surprised concern he quickly added, "Don't worry, he's very tame. He's been around people all his life, and so far nobody's been brave enough to tell him he's not a puppy dog."

The crowd that had gathered laughed a little nervously. Sarah didn't want to seem to be a bad sport, so with a slight lift of her chin she approached the huge animal. In greeting Buford lifted his wide head, touched her cheek with a very wet black nose, and snorted noisily. The crowd laughed again, and the camera kept rolling as the owner proudly stated, "I knew he would like you. He's really very picky about who he kisses."

Sarah took it all in good humor as she wiped off her cheek with one hand and patted the bull's sleek silver gray hump with the other. "I don't usually let a bull kiss me when we first meet, but in Buford's case I'll make an exception," she said, laughing. "What happened to his other horn," she asked, referring to the fact that only one pearly gray horn grew out from the side of his big head.

"He broke it off when he was doing one of his tricks. He wears a falsy when he does professional appearances," his owner explained with a straight face.

Sarah wasn't sure whether or not he was telling the truth, so when she and Tyler were once again heading for the chuck wagon, she asked him, and he assured her that the bull did indeed wear a false horn occasionally.

"I guess all entertainers have their vanities," she joked.

"Did Willie tell you why cows wear bells around their necks?" Tyler asked with a twinkle.

Sarah looked at him suspiciously. She knew that if Willie had said it, it must be strange, but she played along. "No, why?"

"Because their horns don't work," Tyler answered gleefully as Sarah groaned and shook her head.

"I've got to get back to the city. I almost laughed at that one," she retorted as she returned to her trailer so she could wash up before supper.

"Chow's ready. Come and get it," Jed called, banging on the old triangle that hung from his chuck wagon.

Tyler took her arm in an outwardly impersonal gesture, but the gentle squeeze of his fingers told her that his feelings were anything but dispassionate.

This was certainly not the first barbecue Sarah had eaten, but it was a real challenge to try to enjoy the tender, juicy meat that was generously covered with thick, spicy sauce with dozens of curious eyes focused on her. She finally gave up on the ribs entirely and just ate the brisket, which was not as messy. As she was wiping her hands on what was at least her third napkin, an attractive young man she remembered seeing on the trail ride since last Monday came up to her and thrust a crumpled sheet of paper in front of her.

"Excuse me, Miss Day," he murmured shyly. "My name's Dillon Landry, and all week long I've been trying to get up enough nerve to give you this, and it looks like if I don't do it right now, I might not have another chance." He sounded breathless after that rush of words, but his sincere, unconfident voice touched her tender heart.

"What is it?" she asked kindly as she took the paper and opened it, trying to smooth out the wrinkles.

"I write songs. Well, that is, I try to write songs, but I can't get anyone to even look at them. And this one I wrote especially for you. If you should ever want to sing it, I'd be proud to let you have it."

"Would you mind singing it for me?" she questioned gently. "It's difficult to appreciate a song on a cold reading."

"Well, I don't know," he protested doubtfully. "I haven't got my guitar." But no sooner had he spoken than someone handed him a guitar.

"There's never a shortage of guitars on a trail ride," Tyler whispered in her ear. "I know this guy. I've heard him sing before, and he's really good."

And he was. Sarah listened attentively as the young man crooned the words in a soft southern drawl, bringing the guitar strings to life beneath his agile fingers.

"Heaven help me now. I'm lovin' you and how! I've never felt this way; you brighten up my day; can't tear myself away. So Heaven help me now." He repeated the chorus and with a final strum waited expectantly for her response.

When she lifted her eyes, he was startled to see that they were filled with tears. "I'm sorry," he apologized with a crestfallen look on his youthful face. "I didn't realize it was that bad."

"No, no." She shook her head, trying not to break down. "It was very good. And you have a beautiful voice."

"But I didn't mean to make you cry," he moaned.

"You didn't," she tried to reassure him. "I must have gotten a bite of jalapeño pepper by mistake, and it made my eyes water," she lied. "If you're interested, I think I could get you an audition with Mack, my manager. If I know him, he'll probably want to see what else you have and maybe put together a demo record."

"Oh, Miss Day! I can't tell you how great that would be," he exclaimed in astonishment. "Thank you so much. You're really terrific."

"Write your name and telephone number on this piece of paper, and I'll get Mack to call you tomorrow," she promised, handing him back his song. She would give Mack the information, but she would keep that crumpled piece of paper forever. It was like a summary of her week with Tyler and the love she felt for him. Unfortunately her story wouldn't end like the song.

"I really appreciate this." He beamed as he handed the paper back to her.

"It's a tough business," she said, not wanting him to let his hopes get out of hand. "There are thousands of people with beautiful voices and loads of talent that haven't made it. The competition is pretty stiff, but with a little luck and a lot of persistence, you've got what it takes."

"Thanks again," he said, barely containing his excitement as he rushed off to tell his friends the good news.

167

"That was real nice of you," Tyler said warmly.

"It was nothing." She shrugged it off. "His song was really good, and if I didn't think he had a chance, I wouldn't waste Mack's time."

"I know of one young man who won't get any sleep tonight, thinking about tomorrow's phone call," he said, then added in a voice too low for anyone else to hear, "And I know of another not so young man who hopes he won't get any sleep tonight either."

"You're incorrigible," she said, but a merry twinkle in her eyes communicated her approval. She would have to get through the next few hours before she could again be in his arms.

But later, to her surprise, she discovered she was having fun. The country and western band was excellent and the dancing lively as she changed partners too many times to count. She had plenty of opportunities to show off her skill at the Cotton-Eye Joe and the Texas two-step. However, Tyler could be counted on to claim her for every slow dance. Ignoring, for once, their audience, the handsome pair moved as one, their bodies molded together, their steps perfectly matched.

"I feel like I'm cheating on my wife, holding you in public like this." His warm breath tickled her ear. "And I'm not even married. This is the most fun I've ever had with my boots on," he teased.

"It's getting pretty late. It doesn't look like this party is going to break up before dawn." She shivered in delight as he dared to brush a kiss across her temple. "Do you think we would be noticed if we slipped away now?"

"You go first, and then in a few minutes, when I'm sure no one will put two and two together, I'll leave, circle around by the horses, and meet you at your trailer." Suddenly he chuckled. "Now I really feel like I'm cheating on my wife. Here I am setting up a clandestine meeting with a beautiful, desirable woman and almost feeling guilty about it."

"I'll try not to leave any lipstick marks on your collar," she said as her body rubbed sensually against his as they kept time to the music. She, too, felt as if she were competing against another woman, but actually it was a compilation of three women: herself, Sunny, and Tyler's ex-fiancée, and the combination was proving to be too much of a challenge. She clung to him for a moment longer, and then as the song ended she moved away with studied casualness.

The musicians were taking a break, which gave her an opportunity to pass almost unnoticed through the crowd. At the edge of the floodlights she paused for one last lingering look at Tyler's smiling, trusting face with the forelock of black hair falling across his forehead. He lifted his head at that moment, and meeting her eyes across the distance, he spoke to her with a wink more intimate than many kisses she had received from other men. She hoped he knew what a very special man he was and that the woman he finally chose to marry would appreciate and cherish him. Unfortunately, owing to the incredibly bad timing of that rascal Fate, Sarah would never have the opportunity to qualify for that position.

She was so deep in thought as she approached the

169

trailer that she didn't even notice that the lights were on until she tried to unlock the door and discovered that it was already unlocked. Cautiously she stepped into the trailer, ready to flee at the first sign of danger.

"My God, Sarah, I've been waiting for hours. I thought you'd never leave that party," Mack exclaimed as soon as he saw her.

"Mack, what are you doing here?" Sarah asked, relieved it was only him and not some deranged fan. "You scared me to death."

"I've come to take you away from all of this," he stated. "We've got a lot of details to cover before morning, so let's go."

CHAPTER ELEVEN

"We can't go now," Sarah protested frantically. "I was supposed to stay here tonight, then ride in the parade tomorrow."

"Well, that's all been changed. I was able to book Sunny for a couple of last-minute gigs in this area that will fill in the blank time between the parade tomorrow and opening night at the rodeo on Wednesday. Since it might look a little suspicious to have two Sunny Days arrive at the airport within a week of each other, we decided it would be best if she rode in on the bus with the band. And now she's here, and you can be yourself again," Mack explained impatiently.

"But what about the parade?" Sarah repeated. "Who's going to ride in it?"

"Sunny is. She's feeling much better and is ready to get out in public again. Just between you and me, I think she can't stand to remain anonymous for longer than a few hours at a time. She's been driving me crazy for the last few days, and frankly I'm glad this switcheroo is almost over."

"I just can't leave tonight. There are people I still want to see and things I need to do before I go," she persisted.

"You sound like you're fixing to die," Mack said unsympathetically. "Look, it's over. It's time to go back to the real world. Don't be a fool," he added with a spark of insight. "If you've gotten involved with some cowboy, you had to know that it could only last until tomorrow. He thinks you're Sunny Day, the star. Imagine his surprise when he finds out you're Sarah Dayton, the sister." Mack didn't mean to be unkind, but he could be counted on to be bluntly honest, always cutting quickly to the heart of the problem.

"I need time to pack—"

"Your suitcases have already been loaded in the car," he interrupted. "I told you, we're in a hurry. Are you ready to go?"

"Not really, but I guess you're right." Her shoulders slumped dejectedly. "It's over." With one last wistful sigh her gaze flowed around the small trailer, touching fondly on all those places that left her with memories of Tyler.

"I'd better leave a note," she said, stalling, hoping he would return in time for her to say good-bye. "They might worry about me if I just disappear unexpectedly."

"It's all been taken care of. I met some guy named Jeb or Jed or something, and I told him that you needed to leave early but would meet them in the morning just before the parade started. He let me into your trailer and said he would tell everybody else that you had gone."

Everybody else didn't matter . . . just Tyler. But

maybe it was better this way. She wasn't certain she could have handled a drawn-out good-bye, and she didn't want to look ridiculous in front of him. So she would just slip away into the night and hope that Sunny wouldn't say or do something that would make him suspicious. Sarah must get to her and tell her everything . . . well, almost everything.

"Okay, I guess I'm ready," she stated flatly, and followed him to the rental car parked behind the trailer.

During the trip to the hotel she was quiet and sullen. She couldn't shake the feeling that she had been robbed of one last night with Tyler. She could think of dozens of things she would have told him if she had realized they would have no more time together. It was as if she had been awakened abruptly just as she was nearing the climax of a wonderful dream. That was exactly what last week had been—just a dream—and now it was time to wake up. Suddenly all of the lost sleep, the fatigue, and the tension caught up with her, and she felt only a dull, empty numbness.

Mack sensed that something was wrong and tried to start a conversation, but her monosyllabic answers soon discouraged him. Even though it was almost two o'clock in the morning, traffic still whizzed along the Houston freeways, but Sarah didn't notice. Nor did she see the modern office buildings that Tyler, only last Sunday, had told her were a part of the Galleria area as they drove past them.

"Help me watch for my turnoff," Mack directed.

173

"We're staying at a hotel near the Astrodome called the Shamrock Hilton."

"Oh, no, not the Hilton," Sarah said with a groan.

"Why not the Hilton?" he asked, bewildered. "It's convenient, and it's a very nice, old historic hotel that has just recently been completely remodeled. Besides, the Rodeo Association is footing the bill, which makes it even better."

"I'm sure it will be fine." She stared sightlessly out of the window, remembering Tyler's contempt when he had thought she would be disappointed with her accommodations. "It's nothing, really." A lump rose in her throat as giant tears of exhaustion filled her eyes and then flowed unchecked and unnoticed down her cheeks and onto the front of the iridescent blue blouse that Tyler had admired. He had probably already gone to the trailer by now. Or maybe Jed had told him that she had left. She hoped he wasn't hurt by her sudden departure. She had wanted to tell him how much she had enjoyed being with him. It had probably all been just another job to him, but to her it had been special. Everything had ended so abruptly and coldly, so out of keeping with the warm closeness they had shared.

More than likely he would just be angry that they wouldn't be spending the night together. Sarah knew that he cared for her and enjoyed being around her, but men and women seemed to attach different meanings to these very basic feelings. Never had he even hinted that he felt anything other than a sort of wary friendship for her. It didn't occur to her that he, too, had held his emotions in

174

check because of her profession and his own fears. She knew only that he could never have been accused of being anything less than a gentleman. Even on the night of the storm they wouldn't have made love if she hadn't made the first move, however innocent and well-intentioned her motives were. She hadn't left the bedroom thinking that only moments later she would be lying next to his nude body on the sofa, but the results were the same as if she had. No man as healthy and virile as Tyler would turn down a sex-starved female if she offered herself to him.

Her tears of sadness changed to tears of humiliation. Why hadn't she been able to see things this clearly before now? He had done this to her. She couldn't think logically whenever she was close enough to him to see him or smell him or touch him. She had never in her life been the aggressor, especially where men were concerned. It was good that she had left when she had, before she had done or admitted something that she would have been forever embarrassed about.

She could never regret the time they had spent together. It would always be remembered as one of the highlights of her life. A woman always held special memories of the men who had participated in such monumental firsts in her life as her first kiss, her first date, her first love, and her first lover.

"You look awful. Have you been crying?" Sunny commented with concern when Sarah finally arrived in the hotel room and Mack had gone on to his own room.

"I'm just very tired," Sarah offered as an excuse. "I haven't been getting much sleep lately." Half heartedly

175

she discarded the hated wig and slipped out of the blue outfit, accepting the robe that Sunny offered her.

"I think you had better tell me what happened last week, and don't leave anything out. I have a feeling I'm going to meet one unhappy man tomorrow, and I want to be prepared," Sunny said kindly. Because they were twins, they shared a special bond that made them more sensitive to each other's moods than normal sisters, and right now Sunny could feel Sarah's despondency as if it were her own.

The two sisters talked for hours. Sarah told Sunny about all the things she needed to know and the people she had met, particularly those she might have interviews with tomorrow. The parade would be a noisy, impersonal affair that would allow Sunny little time to talk to anyone while they were riding along the actual parade route. And she would make sure that she didn't arrive too early or wait around too long after it was over, so people would have little time to approach her.

Sunny congratulated Sarah on the good job she had done. The press had been positively glowing in their praise of Sarah's performance as Sunny. Her scheduled appearance at the rodeo was enjoying brisk ticket sales and promised to be a near sellout. The masquerade had been a rousing success: Sunny's health and state of mind were restored to normal, and thanks to Sarah her reputation and career had been given a helpful boost.

But when Sarah got to the subject of Tyler, she wasn't sure where to begin, though once started, she couldn't seem to stop. All her joys and fears and the sincere regret that she would never have the chance to see how this relationship would have ended had they met under different circumstances poured out. Even after such a short time her feelings for him were stronger than any she had ever felt for any man before.

Sunny listened and sympathized. She felt responsible for her sister's unhappiness. After all, the switch had been her idea and for her benefit. It had just been one of those awful coincidences that life would choose that particular time to introduce Sarah to a man who could have been her key to happiness. Sunny knew that her sister's loyalties were deep and her affections not easily won. But it was too late and too complicated to help her, wasn't it?

With only three hours of sleep they were both feeling the effects of last night's gab session when they got up that morning. Sunny dressed for the parade and left with Mack while Sarah chose to watch the live broadcast on television.

The announcers were two local newsmen; one she didn't know, but the other was Don Nelson, who had interviewed her for *Good Morning Houston*. Together they kept up a running commentary that was both entertaining and informative as the parade progressed. There seemed to be an extraordinarily large number of local school bands strutting across the small screen. Although they were talented and vivacious, Sarah's eager eyes were waiting for a last look at the one face that had grown so special to her in the last few days. Several floats elaborately decorated with condo-sized cowboy hats and life-size fiberglass horses rolled by before at last she saw him, sitting with some of the other committee chairmen on bales of hay that were placed in a circle around a dance floor on which four couples demonstrated the lively art of square dancing. Like the other chairmen, Tyler was smiling and waving to the thousands of people who lined the downtown streets. He looked incredibly handsome even though he was dressed very simply in a crisp white long-sleeved shirt buttoned at the neck and adorned with a narrow string tie. Tight black western slacks were molded to the muscular shape of his long legs, which were braced against the sway of the float. His gray hat hid most of his thick dark hair and shadowed his eyes, which made it impossible to read his expression. Sarah wondered if he was experiencing any of the same feelings that she was right now. Had he been hurt when he had returned to the trailer and found her already gone, or had he merely been disappointed? She would never know, and possibly it was better that way. Tyler's float passed out of the line of vision of the impersonal lens of the television camera much too quickly as far as Sarah was concerned, but there was still a lot of parade to be seen by others who didn't realize the importance of that one float.

After a few more drill teams, stagecoaches, clowns, and toothy beauty queens performed for the crowds, the trail rides began at last to be announced. It was estimated that there were six to eight thousand riders and horses and approximately two hundred wagons making up the twelve trail rides that stretched back for several miles through the Houston streets.

As the granddaddy of all the trail rides, the Salt Grass

178

Trail Ride led the procession. It was also the largest, with over two thousand riders and thirty-six wagons. Sarah felt an almost maternal pride when it was announced that it had indeed won the outstanding trail ride award. The American and Texas flags were proudly displayed by several wagons, and although many men still sported scraggly week-old beards and everyone showed signs of wear and tear, most of the riders looked clean and happy as they clowned and waved at the cameras. All modern-day conveniences had mysteriously disappeared, giving the impression that these riders had really been roughing it on the trail. There was no sign of the van with the name of a well-known beer prominently displayed on its sides, which had traveled with the trail ride, blaring country and western music from huge speakers, or the flatbed truck with its small village of green portable toilets, which had provided relief to these travelers, who had no other excuse to stop at gasoline stations. And of course no campers or vans were anywhere in sight.

At last Sunny rode into view. Sarah was not really surprised to see that Sunny was seated, not on Zena but on the well-padded seat of a forty-thousand-dollar reproduction stagecoach. It would be interesting to hear how Sunny had talked her way into this unexpected change of transportation. As usual, she looked dazzling, dressed in a tight gold lamé outfit that clung to her like a second skin and sparkled and glittered with an almost blinding brilliance in the bright sun. She waved graciously, throwing kisses and smiling beautifully as the crowd cheered and clapped their approval.

The announcers, too, were full of praise for the publicity Sunny's appearance on the trail ride and in the parade had generated. They informed the audience that over six hundred thousand people were expected to attend this year's rodeo, which was considerably more than last year. They also volunteered the information that Gene Autry had been the first star entertainer at the Houston Rodeo in 1942, replacing such exciting acts as trick horses, concerts, and dog races.

Sunny's protective circle of cowboys finally moved on, and Sarah searched out the other familiar faces from among the thousands of urban, drugstore, and, most rare, real cowboys and cowgirls that filed past. There was Willie, riding old Ethyl, of course, and Jed, driving the chuck wagon. The newly married couple whose wedding she had attended last evening were conspicuous with their horses decorated with bells and ribbons woven into their manes and tails and signs saying "Just" attached to the bride's back and "Married" to the groom's.

After every other trail ride several green street-cleaning machines went by, attempting to keep the animal deposits under control. Someone commented that today there was enough horse manure on these streets to grow roses in the concrete. The announcers also said that although Harris County was almost entirely urban, it had a larger horse population than any other county in the United States. In fact, there were more horses and riders in this one area than there had been at any other time in all of Texas. Horses did seem to be the most popular way to travel, although a few unorthodox and daring cowboys

180

rode on saddled longhorn steers, stick horses, and even one shaggy dark brown buffalo. Buford, too, put in an appearance, with his false horn and three children and a dog balanced on his broad back.

It had been years since Sarah had actually attended a parade, and she had certainly never been to one of the same magnitude as this one. She watched the rest of the parade with increasing depression. It only served to make her more aware that this last week had been like a childhood fantasy. None of it had been real, including Tyler. It was time she turned her thoughts again to her future and tried to forget the past.

"You mean that even after last week you still want to leave me and the tour and go vegetate on some little farm in Kentucky?" Sunny asked incredulously later that afternoon as she dressed for the performance that had been scheduled by Mack for that evening.

"Especially after last week," Sarah answered firmly. "I'll never understand how you can stand all that attention day after day, year after year. It nearly drove me crazy."

"I honestly don't think I could live without it. Doing nothing for a week nearly drove *me* crazy!" The two sisters smiled, understanding each other's feelings but not sharing ambitions. It would be a difficult adjustment for both of them, because they had always been very close. But Sunny knew Sarah well enough to know that once she had made up her mind, there was really no use in trying to talk her out of it. And Sarah knew Sunny well enough to know that she would try anyway, but she remained firm in her decision.

"I'm singing at a club in Galveston tonight, and we'll probably go out for a good dinner afterward. You'd better hurry up and get dressed because we have to leave in a few minutes," Sunny reminded Sarah.

"I think I'll just stay here and go to bed early. I have several nights of sleep to catch up on," Sarah answered, stretching lazily. Maybe if she weren't so tired, she wouldn't feel such an apathy toward life.

Sunny started to tease her sister about the reasons for her lack of sleep but snapped her mouth shut. Sarah hadn't shared any of the intimate details of her relationship with that cowboy named Tyler, but she had said that he was really someone special. Sunny sensed that it was a very personal thing and that Sarah wouldn't appreciate being kidded about it, especially right now.

Sunny's concern for her sister grew as she watched her mope around for the next three days. It seemed to take all of Sarah's energy each day to get out of bed and get dressed. Sunny and Mack even insisted that Sarah accompany them on a sight-seeing and shopping tour of Houston, but even though she was with them physically, it was obvious her thoughts were somewhere else. Sunny was convinced that Sarah needed a change of scenery, and she was looking forward to leaving Houston after tomorrow night's rodeo performance.

As she was getting ready to leave for the other club date Mack had set up, Sunny tried again to get Sarah to join them, but Sarah offered some excuse about watching an old movie on TV. "I really wish you'd change your mind," Sunny persisted. "This place is only a few miles from here, and I promise that we'll come right back after my show. Mack said this was a new club, and even though Alvin is not a very big town, he said everybody seemed real nice and—"

"You're singing at a club in Alvin?" Sarah interrupted.

Encouraged by her sudden interest but a little confused, Sunny nodded. "They're not usually open on weeknights, but since this was the only time I could—"

"I'll just be a minute," Sarah interrupted again as she jumped up and almost ran into her room, with Sunny's bewildered gaze following her.

The ride to Alvin didn't take long, but by the time they pulled into the parking lot, Sarah's nerves were stretched as tight as guitar strings. This was Tyler's hometown, and maybe, just maybe, he would come to hear Sunny sing tonight. Sarah had missed him so much that with the least encouragement she could possibly even get up the nerve to walk right up to him and tell him the truth. Before the show began, she paced backstage like a caged tiger, until Mack forced her to sit in a chair just offstage because she was making everyone else nervous. It was a good location from which to observe without being seen, so she stayed there during Sunny's entire set. As always, the room soon filled with smoke, and although the customers stopped dancing while Sunny was singing, there was still a steady clink of beer bottles and cans being passed and put down on the Formica tabletops.

Sarah's eyes ached from the effort of trying to see

183

through the haze and single out the one person she wanted to see in the semidarkness. She recognized several people who had been on the trail ride, but Tyler wasn't one of them. If possible, she was even more dejected than before as she rode back to the hotel later that night.

"Did you see him?" Sunny asked perceptively.

"Who?" Sarah answered evasively.

"Whoever you were looking for so hard that your eyes are as bloodshot as if you had been on a two-week drunk. Does Tyler live in Alvin? That would certainly explain your sudden change of heart when I told you where I'd be singing tonight."

"I thought he might show up," Sarah admitted in a small, sad voice. "But it obviously wasn't important enough for him to come tonight."

"When I met him Saturday at the parade, he acted really distant," Sunny told her.

"What did he say? Did he ask why I had left early?" Sarah asked, hungry for any details about him.

"Not really. After I told him I had decided to accept the offer to ride on that stagecoach instead of on horse-back, an offer for which I am eternally grateful," Sunny added as she strayed from the original subject, "he just turned and left me standing there. He had a chip on his shoulder as big as Texas. I admit he was really a handsome hunk of mucho macho, but he wasn't very friendly. I like my men a little more attentive and adoring."

"He can be all that and more," Sarah whispered. "I just wish that I had met him at some other place and under different circumstances, so I would know for sure. We never really had a chance."

That night Sarah tossed and turned, troubled by choppy, exhausting dreams. Even without the strains of reveille to announce the dawn, she had been waking each morning in time to watch the sun rise behind the unique Houston skyline. She had never had trouble sleeping, but now she just felt so alone. It was strange that her body had become so addicted to sleeping next to Tyler's after just two nights together that she could miss his warmth and strength.

At last, after sitting at the hotel room window and watching the city come back to life as people jammed the streets going to work, she forced herself to go back to bed and get a few more hours of sleep. It was almost noon when she woke again, and she felt much better. But it left her with very few hours to get everything packed in time for a smooth exit from the city after tonight's rodeo performance.

As she, Sunny, and Mack rode to the Astrodome in the long black limousine that had been sent for them, she even felt enough like her old self to ask Mack how Dillon Landry's audition had gone. Mack was enthusiastic about Dillon's prospects and anxious to get a demo record cut. Sarah smiled to herself. Things were returning to normal. Sunny was Sunny, dressed in her elaborate blond wig, her flashy stage costume, and dramatic makeup, while Sarah was Sarah, with her long honey-blond hair flowing freely down her back and dressed in faded fitted jeans, a blue chambray shirt, and wearing just a light touch of makeup.

"This is the way to travel," Sunny said with a sigh, leaning back against the plush velvet-covered seat. "Four wheels beats four legs any day. I hope I never have to ride on another horse again. Mack, make sure that you add a clause to that effect in all my future contracts."

Sarah, of course, didn't agree, but she didn't argue. Thinking of horses made her think of Tyler, although he never seemed to be far from her thoughts. She knew that she should be trying to forget him, but he was still so fresh in her mind. She cherished her time with him. Without him there would always be a special emptiness that could never be filled by another man, but maybe soon all the sharp edges of her memories would smooth over, so that she wouldn't be choked by this lump in her throat.

The limousine entered the Astrodome through a special entrance, stopping right by Sunny's dressing room. Sarah helped her sister put on the final touches, then followed her out to wait for Sunny's big introduction.

"And now, ladies and gentlemen," the PA system blared, *"here's the little lady you've all been waiting for. Let's give a big Houston welcome to Miss Sunny Day!!!"*

Sunny rode into the arena, perched prettily on the back of an open convertible, and made a slow circle around the ring before joining her band on a revolving platform in the middle of the Astrodome. The cowboys who had been hanging around the bucking chutes checking their equipment and waiting their turn to ride the broncs or the bulls or rope calves dropped everything and hurried to the fence so they could watch Sunny in action.

Sarah, too, moved toward the arena, then climbed up on one of the gates so she could get a better view of her sister. This was probably the last performance she would see for some time. She was listening to Sunny's version of "Mommas, Don't Let Your Babies Grow Up to Be Cowboys" when a deep voice behind her asked, "How much longer is this performance going to last?"

"Sunny's shows always run about forty-five minutes," she answered automatically, without looking over her shoulder.

"That wasn't the performance I meant, Sarah," the voice responded.

It took a second for her to register that the man had used her name—and then she realized that she knew that voice. Whirling around, she lost her balance and started to fall backward off the tall wooden gate.

Tyler caught her, cradling her in his arms for just a moment before he let her slide safely to the ground. Her knees threatened to buckle beneath her as she stared wide-eyed at the closed, unfriendly expression on his beloved face.

"You were full of pretty words last week," he mocked. "What's the matter? Cat got your tongue?"

"When you're in it up to your nose, keep your mouth shut," she flashed back, her whole body trembling so violently that she thought she would shake apart.

He didn't smile, but a tiny twinkle flickered briefly in his solemn gray eyes before it was abruptly extinguished.

187

"Is there anything you'd like to tell me? Maybe about your family," he prompted.

"I have a sneaking suspicion that there's not much I could tell you that you don't already know," she answered, then started to turn back toward the arena. "You're missing Sunny's show."

"I don't give a damn about Sunny's show," he exploded, roughly grabbing her arm and turning her around to face him. "I want an explanation. I want to know why you didn't tell me the truth last week?"

"Why should I have? What guarantees did I have that you wouldn't run to the press?" she flared back in a whisper so no one would overhear more than they should. "What are you going to do now that you know our little secret?"

"Why couldn't you trust me?" His voice was ragged. "I couldn't believe you had run away without so much as a word of good-bye. You didn't even leave a note."

Sarah hesitated. Had it really meant something special to him, or had his feelings just been hurt by the deception? It was important to her to know, but from his attitude she could tell that all he wanted from her now was an explanation. Then he would probably walk out of her life forever. Her chin lifted defiantly as she spoke. "I don't owe you anything. You never led me to believe that you wanted any more from me than a few nights of diversion. But I'm not complaining. I got my money's worth."

"You know it was more than that," he said angrily. "I never meant for it to happen, and God knows, I fought against it, but we were good together."

"There's more to life than sex," she retorted.

"Damn it, I didn't mean that we were good together just in bed." He spat the words out between clenched teeth. The muscle in his jaw twitched as he struggled for control. When he spoke again, his voice was softer and strangely vulnerable.

"As soon as I realized what kind of person you were underneath those gaudy wigs and flashy clothes, I knew what I was feeling for you was more than I should. But I didn't want to get involved with a woman who would be on the road most of the time. I couldn't see myself following you from club to club, burning with jealousy every time a man got a little out of line with you."

"You could have told me that," she murmured.

"And you could have told me who you were. You must have gotten a big laugh out of how well you fooled me."

"No, I hated every minute of it. But I had promised my sister, and she had so much at stake." Suddenly Sarah frowned. "Who told you the truth, anyway?"

"Your sister decided to play cupid. She called me this morning and told me that if I was half as miserable as you were, we probably deserved each other. She explained the whole situation and told me it was all her fault and that she would never forgive herself if you vegetated alone in Kentucky when you could vegetate with me in Alvin. I wasn't absolutely sure what she meant, but I got the gist of it. She was really worried about you."

"She should have told me she talked to you," Sarah stated, her bravado completely deflated.

"What would you have done then?"

"Probably nothing. I figured that you'd be so furious you wouldn't ever speak to me again anyway."

"You've got that right!" he exclaimed roughly, but his gray eyes softened as he looked at her with undisguised longing. "Except for the part about me never speaking to you again. I was so mad I could have strangled you with my bare hands for what you put me through. But then I decided that I'd give it one last shot before I gave up on ever seeing you again."

"But what about your ex-fiancée?" she asked timidly.

"My what?"

"The girl who lied to you about her modeling job and had the abortion."

"That was years ago." He looked straight into Sarah's eyes as he continued. "I was much younger and much dumber. I never really loved her, or we would have been able to work things out. You and she are not at all similar."

"I was so afraid that you wouldn't understand that I couldn't tell you how I felt. Besides, I had never felt this way before and wasn't too sure of my own reactions," she whispered, her gaze locked with his. "It was all happening too fast. I've never been in love before. . . ."

"And you would have sacrificed your own chance of happiness for your sister," he muttered, his voice filled with a grudging respect. "My proud, loyal little star," he said, reaching out and pulling her trembling body into the protection of his strong arms. Joyfully he buried his face in the sweet-smelling cloud of her golden hair.

"I missed you so much," she whispered. "I didn't real-

190

ize how much I cared for you until I didn't think I would ever see you again."

"The last few days haven't been much fun for me either," he admitted. "Do you think we could start over, and maybe this time we would get it right?"

Her face lit by a happy smile, she pulled away from him and extended her hand. "Hello, my name is Sarah Dayton, and I'm just a country girl from Kentucky."

"Well, maybe we could skip a few parts in between." He laughed and pulled her willing body back into an affectionate bear hug.